W9-AFY-522

J FIC SMI

Smith, Clete Barrett
Aliens in disguise

...mo Branch Library
...6251 St. Andrews Road
Columbia, SC 29212

Also by Clete Barrett Smith

Aliens on Vacation

Alien on a Rampage

Aliens in Disguise

Aliens in Disguise

by Clete Barrett Smith
illustrated by Christian Slade

Disney • Hyperion Books
New York

Text copyright © 2013 by Clete Barrett Smith
Illustrations copyright © 2013 by Christian Slade

All rights reserved. Published by Disney • Hyperion Books, an
imprint of Disney Book Group. No part of this book may be
reproduced or transmitted in any form or by any means, electronic or
mechanical, including photocopying, recording, or by any information
storage and retrieval system, without written permission from
the publisher. For information address Disney • Hyperion Books,
114 Fifth Avenue, New York, New York 10011-5690.

First Edition

Printed in the United States of America

1 3 5 7 9 10 8 6 4 2

G475-5664-5 -13046

Reinforced binding

Library of Congress Cataloging-in-Publication Data
Smith, Clete Barrett.
Aliens in disguise/by Clete Barrett Smith;
illustrated by Christian Slade.—1st ed.
p. cm.—(The Intergalactic Bed & Breakfast)
Summary: When a pair of UFO-watchers disguised as aliens tries
to get inside the Intergalactic Bed & Breakfast to broadcast their
findings, it is up to David and Amy to keep the imposters at bay.
ISBN 978-1-4231-6598-9
[1. Extraterrestrial beings—Fiction.   2. Impersonation—Fiction.
3. Bed and breakfast accommodations—Fiction.   4. Science fiction.]
I. Slade, Christian, ill.   II. Title.
PZ7.S644633Ale 2013
[Fic]—dc22   2012019758

Visit www.disneyhyperionbooks.com

SUSTAINABLE FORESTRY INITIATIVE   Certified Sourcing
www.sfiprogram.org
SFI-00993

THIS LABEL APPLIES TO TEXT STOCK

For Logan and Weenz
(But mostly for Weenz, obviously)

1

It was the perfect evening. Picnic blanket. Fried summer food. Coolest girl on the planet beside me.

Our hilltop spot gave us a panoramic view of Forest Grove. And when the sun disappeared in a blaze of those colors you only find in sunsets, it left the night sky wide open for the fireworks show.

Splat!

A gob of warm slime smacked me in the forehead and oozed down my cheek.

Correction. It was *almost* the perfect evening.

At least for a few minutes I had been able to forget that

Amy and I were supervising a field trip of rowdy kids from outer space. It was just another one of our weird jobs as employees of Grandma's Intergalactic Bed & Breakfast.

"Oh, I do apologize." Mrs. Crowzen, their teacher—the only other chaperone helping us watch these eight alien delinquents—rushed over, waving a hanky in her spindly claw. She reached down to wipe the slime from my face, but I held up my hands, fending her off. Her body was covered in crunchy exoskeleton plates, kind of like a crab's, which meant she was pretty clueless about the sensitivity of human skin. The last time she "helped" clean me up, I swear she almost rubbed hard enough to scrape down to the bone.

"It's okay, I got it." I dragged my palm across my cheek and then wiped it on the ground, leaving a bright yellowish-green streak on the grass. It looked like the aftermath of the world's messiest sneeze.

"Don't worry about it, Mrs. Crowzen," Amy said, giving me a mischievous grin. "David looks much better this way."

I scooped more slime off my face and flicked my fingers, splattering Amy with flecks of space goop.

"Gross!"

"Hey, you're the one who wants to study everything about aliens." I flicked more snotty-drops at her. "I'm just giving you some free samples." Amy smacked me on the shoulder, hard; then we both burst out laughing.

Mrs. Crowzen raked her claws along her chest plate in a well-practiced motion, grating against a patch of little bumps to make an unpleasant screeching that instantly got the kids' attention. "Boys! You get over here this instant!"

A pair of little aliens shuffled forward, heads bowed. They

actually looked pretty humanoid, aside from the antennae and the whole drenched-in-slime thing. As obnoxious as they were, I almost felt bad for these two. Earth's atmosphere was too humid for their bodies, causing the endless slime excretion. Maybe it was like sweating and it kept them from overheating or something. Whatever the explanation, it didn't make it any less gross.

"You two owe our gracious hosts an apology." The teacher gestured at Amy and me.

"But it's not our fault! It feels like I'm walking around in a bowl of glicklespitz soup on this planet." One of the little aliens held up a hand that was dripping trails of goop.

"We're not *trying* to do any of this. It just happens. Look." The other one shook his body like a wet dog, and goo drop-lets sprayed everywhere. Amy and I yanked the blanket over our legs to avoid getting splattered again. It might have passed for an innocent mistake...but I caught the second alien hiding a grin.

So did Mrs. Crowzen. "Nonsense," the teacher said, grabbing an antenna on top of each of their heads, twisting them until those little smiles turned into grimaces, and then marching the kids toward the rest of the group. "You have been deliberately throwing clumps of secretion at each other ever since we arrived. And now you have soiled one of our hosts."

"Again," Amy whispered, elbowing me in the ribs and snickering.

"But we didn't mean to—"

"You are going to behave like proper guests on this planet. Sit down and wait for the sky show." The aliens trudged down the line of blankets to where the other kids sat. "On *opposite* sides, if you please." The boys split up and slumped onto the grass on either side of the crowd.

The otherworldly students were decked out in corny stars-and-stripes-themed paper hats and T-shirts to hide scales and extra limbs and neon skin colors. It worked from a distance, especially in the fading light. But it was far from the perfect disguise. Up close, they basically looked like the most patriotic group of space aliens in the galaxy.

The PA system crackled to life down in the park. "Happy Fourth of July, Forest Grove," the mayor's voice boomed out through the speakers. I'm sure it was really loud down there, a safe distance from our little alien outing, but up on the hill the words were faint. "The fireworks display will start in five minutes." A cheer drifted up from the crowd.

I stole a glance at Amy. She was watching the sky, eyes shining with excitement. But if I knew her, she was more interested in the constellations than the pyrotechnics. I scooched a little closer. Maybe I could put my arm around—

"AAAAAAHHHHHH!" I yelled (no, it was *not* a scream, thankyouverymuch) as the picnic blanket came to life and jumped onto my lap.

Amy glanced over. "What are you screaming about?" she said. "It's just Kanduu."

"That wasn't a scream." I mentally ditched my plans to get closer to her, and sighed. "Hi, Kanduu." The kid alien was only about two feet tall and had color-changing skin like a chameleon. Who knows how long he'd been lurking there, blending in with the red-and-white-checkered pattern of the blanket, just waiting to scare me. It had been his favorite activity since arriving on the planet.

As Kanduu stood on my lap, his skin faded into the color of my old blue jeans. His class was from an inter-solar-system school made up of kids from different planets, so at least he didn't have the slime problem. Kanduu put his tiny hands on my chest and leaned forward until his squishy nose touched mine. "Greetings, earthling. Take me to your leader."

Kanduu fell back on the blanket and rolled around, his laughter a series of honking noises. He'd heard that phrase in an old cartoon during one of Amy's Movie Nights, and he thought it was hilarious. Just like all of his alien classmates. As if such a primitive planet as Earth could actually have leaders.

"Amy's the leader around here," I said, scooping the little guy up and dumping him on Amy's lap. He cuddled into her arms and blended into her pink sweatshirt until they looked like one being.

I leaned over and grabbed a fried treat from the basket. The food was still warm—I had stocked up at the snack stands in the park while Amy herded the alien kids.

Kanduu sniffed the air. "What is that?"

"This, my friend, is a corn dog." I raised it by its stick handle. "Pretty much the perfect food."

Kanduu's spongy face scrunched up in disgust.

"What's the matter?"

He gestured down the hill, where little kids were running around with dogs on the edge of the crowd. "Humans eat their pets?"

"What? No. No, it's not a real dog. It's just called that."

Kanduu tilted his little head. "So... humans think that sounds tasty? To name foodstuffs after their cute little domesticated life companions?"

"I guess." I suppose it did sound a little gross when you thought of it like that.

He pointed. "And then they impale the 'dog' on a piece of wood?"

I shrugged. "Everything tastes better on a stick. Trust me. It's an Earth thing."

He sniffed again. "My sensors inform me that this *dog* is a highly processed product made from the questionable parts of several different Earth beasts." One more sniff. "Nutritional value: dubious at best."

"Sure, but it's a holiday. Food isn't bad for you if you eat it on a holiday."

"Really?"

"All humans know this. Eating large quantities of unhealthy food is pretty much the basis of all our holiday activities."

Kanduu grabbed his little notebook and furiously scribbled some notes. Each night the kids had to write a report on the things they had learned about Earth that day.

Amy glanced over. "Don't write that down, Kanduu. He's teasing you."

I dunked the end of the corn dog into a puddle of ketchup on a paper plate.

"What's that?" Kanduu asked.

I was getting tired of defending my planet's food customs to a judgmental second grader. "Blood," I said, then made crazy eyes and took a big bite.

"Eeeewwwwww!" Kanduu ducked his head and peered at me from beneath Amy's arm.

I licked the ketchup from the corners of my mouth. "Dog's blood."

"YUCK!" Kanduu covered his eyes and buried himself in Amy's sweatshirt.

Amy swatted at my arm. "Stop scaring the poor thing."

"Oh, I'm not scared." Kanduu popped right back up like a prairie dog. "Can I try a bite?"

Amy rolled her eyes. "I guess boys are boys, no matter what planet they're from."

"You leave our hosts alone now," Mrs. Crowzen called from her position in the middle of the students behind us.

"It's okay," I said over my shoulder, offering Kanduu a bite. He chewed thoughtfully, looking maybe a little disappointed that it wasn't totally disgusting.

Patriotic music blared from the PA speakers as the first firework streaked into the sky. The crowd cheered when it burst into a colorful shower of sparks. And then the show was on, one firework after another, sometimes four or five at the same time, a *Boom!* echoing a few seconds after each explosion.

Amy applauded, her face beaming in the rainbow glow. "The Fourth of July show always makes me feel like a little girl again."

Huge pinwheels of color filled the sky. Shadows swirled up and down the surrounding trees, making the forest seem alive, like a group of giants enjoying the show. For a small town on the outskirts of Nowhere, Washington, it was actually a pretty impressive display.

Kanduu hopped onto my lap and tapped my chest. "This is it?" he asked. "This is what we were waiting all evening for?"

"Yep. Humans think this is pretty cool." Sometimes it's hard to impress aliens. Most come to Earth to get away from it all, to "rough it" without any super-advanced technology. The fireworks probably seemed quaint at best. "What's the matter—not what you were expecting?"

"It's not that. I just thought it kind of looked like—" He broke off and scanned the surrounding grass. "Here, let me show you." Kanduu jumped from my lap—he was so light that the feeling barely registered—and stalked around the blanket.

"What are you doing?"

He held a finger up to his mouth hole (he didn't really have what you could call lips) in the human gesture for *Quiet!* that Amy had taught him. Then he straightened up and pointed at the ground. "There she is!"

I squinted, but I only saw a mound of grass. With a closer look, though, I noticed that the mound was shivering all over.

Kanduu bent down and talked to the lump. "I knew my sensors were detecting you. Come on, get up."

The mound arose and unfurled itself into the shape of Kanduu's little sister, Kandeel. She was even tinier than he was, and her skin mimicked the grass perfectly—not just the color but also the pattern of the individual blades. I could have looked all night and not found her.

She glanced up at me, then lowered her eyes and scurried back toward her classmates.

"Wait up," her brother said, grabbing her by the arm and pulling her back to our blanket. "I want you to show him the beacon." She resisted, but Kanduu was stronger, and Kandeel's feet slid across the grass. "You know, the one Mom made us bring."

Kandeel eyed me warily, and when they got close she wrenched free of her brother's grip and hid behind Amy, who was still watching the sky. Amy put her arm around the little girl alien.

"I don't know why she likes you so much better," I muttered.

"My guess would be your shirt."

"What's wrong with my shirt?"

"They can probably smell it from their home planet." Amy wrinkled her nose. "You wear it every day and I bet you haven't washed it in a week. I can't believe you didn't bring more clothes for a two-month stay."

I sniffed the shirt. "Come on, it's not that bad. Besides, it's okay to wear the same clothes in the summer. The rules are different on vacation."

Kanduu scribbled in his notebook.

"Don't write that one down, either," Amy said.

Kanduu set the notebook aside. "Come on, show us the beacon, Kandeel." His sister peeked out at us from behind Amy. "Just come here. Right over to the blanket." Kanduu said it soothingly, beckoning to her. "Please?"

Kandeel crept forward. The instant her foot hit the blanket, her entire body went red-and-white checks all over. Man, she was even better at that than her brother.

"Show him the beacon," Kanduu repeated.

Kandeel studied me with the look of a small animal frozen by fear. When she finally spoke, her voice was a squeak, nearly drowned out by the popping of the fireworks. "Mom said it's only for emergencies."

"But I just want to show him one time. Come on, it's way cooler than those fireworks."

Like her brother's, Kandeel's body was segmented. You know those stacking baby toys that are a series of increasingly smaller circles on a little plastic dowel? The two of them looked sort of like that. She dug her fingers in between two of the segments that made up her torso and withdrew a silver cylinder about the size of a bullet.

Uh-oh. Off-world tech. I instantly went cold all over. The last time an alien gadget was smuggled here—earlier this summer—it had nearly destroyed the entire planet. I stopped the whole thing from happening by...Well, that's a story for another time.

"What is that?" My throat had gone so dry that the words came out in a croak.

"It's a beacon. You know, a signal?" Kanduu said.

"Why don't you hand that over? Right now, okay?"

Kandeel shot me a mistrustful look and took a few steps backward. "Our mom gave it to us in case we got lost. So Teacher could find us." She lowered her eyes, talking to the ground. "It's our first time on another planet."

Kanduu snorted and shook his head in disgust. "Mom worries too much. Give it here."

He grabbed for the device, but Kandeel whisked it out of range. The chase was on as he lunged for her and she ran in circles around the blanket.

Terrified that they were going to set it off—whatever

it was; I didn't know what the word *beacon* might mean to aliens—I scrambled after them on all fours. But it was already pretty dark, and they had assumed the color of the grass, so it probably looked like I was frantically galloping around the blanket all by myself. The crowd of alien kids pointed and buzzed with space laughter. Not my finest moment.

"What are you doing?" Amy finally pried her eyes away from the fireworks show.

"They've got a little device of some kind. Looks metalish."

Amy's eyes went wide—it didn't take her long to remember the doomsday device our former handyman had carried in his coveralls. So she joined me in scampering around the blanket. At least I had some company in looking like a moron.

Music from the PA system swelled to a crescendo, and the crowd sang along with the part about the bombs bursting in air. The timing of the overhead explosions ramped up, rapid-fire, like a string of enormous firecrackers. We were missing the big finale.

Kandeel and her brother jumped back onto the blanket and stood out against the night sky in red-and-white checks. Amy and I pounced at the same time and got tangled up.

"*...does that star-spangled banner yet wa—ave...*"

Kanduu grabbed at the silver device. Kandeel spun away, but it slipped out of her fingers and landed on the blanket. I snatched it up—but, man, was it slick. The little thing squirted right out of my fingers and ricocheted off Amy's forehead.

"Ow!"

"*...the laaaaand of the free—eee...*"

The four of us froze as we scanned the blanket, searching for the beacon. There! Right in the middle of our little circle. We all dove for it at the same time and ended up in a dog pile.

Kanduu got his tiny fingers around it first, slipped out from under us, and ran several yards away from the blanket.

I lifted myself up to my knees. "Kanduu, please don't—"

"...*home of the BRAVE!*"

The biggest firework of the night went off with a circle of fire that lit up the whole town for a moment. The crowd cheered. The Forest Grove fireworks show was over.

The Intergalactic Bed & Breakfast show, however, was not.

Kanduu pressed a little button, which made a metallic *click*.

A tiny orb of light shot from the tip, streaked toward the stars, and expanded. In an instant, the entire night sky was glowing. The light started out like a second moon, but grew stronger until it was as bright as noontime, then got so dazzling it was almost painful, like when someone shines a flashlight right in your face. In a few moments it was so intense that I wondered crazily if the sun was going to crash right into the Earth, and I threw my arms over my face to protect my eyes.

The crowd below gasped in unison.

When the light dimmed enough to allow me to open my eyes, I saw that the scattered clouds were all crackling with electricity, each one hosting a tiny storm surrounded by a swirl of sparks. Then a bolt of lightning shot out of each cloud and converged in the middle of the sky, melding into a huge mass of white-hot energy, a hundred times bigger than that final human firework, churning in a massive whirlpool like the lost arm of some exotic galaxy.

It looked like the end of the world.

I tore my eyes away from the sky and looked for Amy. Every one of her hairs was standing straight up on her head. I felt a sudden need to grab her, protect her, but what would I even be able to do?

Zzzzzt!

The great lightning mass contracted into a tiny silver orb with a sizzle and dropped out of the sky, right back into the little silver cylinder. The night went dark again.

Kanduu spread out his palms and shrugged. "Our mom's a little overprotective."

"She wanted Teacher to be able to see the light, wherever we were," Kandeel squeaked. "In case we got lost."

Mrs. Crowzen clicked her claws together angrily. "I certainly did see it, and the beacon is not a toy. Put it away this instant."

I gulped. "I think my friends back in Florida could see that." Turning to Mrs. Crowzen, I said, "Are their parents going to show up now?" I shuddered just thinking about it. The one night a year when the entire town was outside staring at the sky together would probably not be the best time for the arrival of an angry alien family.

But the teacher just shook her head. "The beacon is only used to help me pinpoint a lost child's location on the planet."

Well, it was certainly effective. Down in Forest Grove, the crowd was motionless, soundless. Every head was craned to gape at the suddenly empty sky.

Amy grabbed my arm. She tried to say something, but

panic had taken her voice. She mouthed, "What are we going to do?"

I did not have a good answer. Or even a bad one. Our job was to keep everything at the B&B a secret, but how could we possibly explain away a sight like *that*?

Just then something happened. Someone down in the park let out a great *Woo-hoo!* Then the clapping started. And the cheering. And lots more woo-hooing.

Phew! The crowd must have thought it had just seen the greatest fireworks finale in the history of the town.

The mayor's somewhat confused voice came over the loudspeaker. "I, uh, suppose *that* concludes the show. Happy Fourth of July, folks."

The cheering intensified. The whole crowd was ecstatic. Kanduu's little device had whipped them into a patriotic fervor. If the entire British army had marched into town just then with their red coats and cannons, the citizens of Forest Grove would have put up a heck of a fight. The Battle of Corn Dog Hill.

Amy exhaled slowly as the color returned to her face. "That was a close one."

"Yeah." I stood up, legs shaky from the relief of dodging yet another bullet. "Let's get everyone back inside before something really noticeable happens."

We helped Mrs. Crowzen round up her students and march them single file back to the B&B. No one wanted to be next to the slime drippers, so those two brought up the rear.

Amy carried Kanduu and Kandeel in the crook of each arm, gently explaining the importance of secrecy while on Earth, and reminding them to leave any off-world gadgets in their rooms. I was glad she was around for stuff like that. I seriously doubt I could have stayed so calm.

It was hard just to be civil to all these kids sometimes, especially in the evening. They basically messed around all day—just like Earth kids—and when it was almost time to write their reports they swarmed around me, firing off a million questions like miniature investigative journalists at the world's weirdest press conference. Kanduu's were always the worst, because they set off such wild speculation among his classmates.

"Don't you think it's weird that everyone on this planet wears clothes all the time?"

"Yeah, what kind of strange custom is that?"

"It's totally confusing!"

"How can you even tell who is a boy and who is a girl?"

I mean, how was I supposed to answer something like that?

This was the second summer I had worked at Grandma's inn for space aliens—the only place of its kind in the whole world—but I still didn't feel like humanity's best choice for ambassador to the rest of the universe. Grandma and Amy were better at all that interspecies-relations stuff. I just wanted to help keep the business running, which meant that my most important job was usually preventing anyone from Forest Grove (or anywhere else) from learning about the biggest secret on the planet.

And right now, that meant getting everybody safely back inside after the incident with the beacon. We came upon other space Tourists on the way back, adult guests who had spread out their blankets a good distance away from all the noisy kids. Amy set Kanduu and his sister down to rejoin the class, and then we both lagged behind to help the older Tourists pack up and to make sure that everyone was headed to Grandma's.

"I always get nervous when they're outside without their full earthling disguises," I said.

"I know. But it's dark, and this is a pretty secluded spot." Amy gestured all around us at the grassy hilltop, surrounded on three sides by dense forest. "And we've always got our emergency alibi."

"I hope that works." If anyone from town caught a glimpse of an undisguised alien, our story would be that the Intergalactic Bed & Breakfast was hosting a sci-fi costume party and some of the guests had gotten lost. Every once in a while we even put up posters around town advertising an "Alien Masquerade Ball" for added authenticity. They never included a time or date for the event, of course.

It was as good an excuse as any, and actually pretty believable. Amy's dad—he used to be sheriff and was now in charge of security at Grandma's—had come up with that one. "It'll work because the townsfolk already think a space-themed inn is half bonkers, anyway," Tate often said. Then, under his breath, he'd add something like, "They're almost right. This place is certified one thousand percent bonkers."

Tate was usually pretty grumpy like that. If it were up to him, the vacationing aliens would never leave the premises after showing up in the guest room closets (which were actually interstellar transporters). As much as I hated to admit it, though, he was probably a good person to have around to counterbalance Grandma. She had been hanging out with the aliens for so long, she tended to forget that anyone else might find them strange.

And speaking of strange... "Amy, look over there." I

swept my flashlight along the path. "Does that look like what I think it looks like?"

A group of adult aliens was being herded into formation, four of them crouching down in front and three standing tall in back, almost as if they were . . .

"They're not seriously trying to take some kind of group picture," Amy said. "Are they?"

Not good. The rules were clear at the B&B: no off-world tech, and definitely no pictures.

We hurried down the path. A pair of aliens was organizing the crowd—the male was lanky and made loose-limbed movements as he waved the other aliens into position, while the female was short and stout, bustling around the edges of the group. The moonlight revealed that they both had pointy ears of a deep blue that didn't quite match the more aqua tone of the rest of their skin. Maybe their species stored extra water in the earlobes or something.

"You look fantastic," the male said. "Everybody smile big!"

Amy and I reached the group just as all the aliens flashed their best smiles. Yikes. That could get a little strange. Like the frog-faced dude in the back—with his wide, wet lips and double rows of sharp teeth, his "smile" made him look capable of biting someone's arm off.

The gangly blue-skinned male with the mismatched ears pulled something out of his pocket and pointed it at the group.

"Wait!" I reached out and grabbed his shoulder. "What is that thing?"

He flinched and whipped his head around. His eyes went

wide for a moment, then he calmed down, shrugged, and showed me what he had.

I was expecting another piece of advanced alien technology, but I got a surprise. "That's just a phone," I said. "A regular Earth phone."

The male raised his blue eyebrows and exchanged some sort of meaningful glance with his little round mate. Were they communicating telepathically? Nothing much about aliens would surprise me anymore.

"Where did you get that?" Amy said.

"Oh, I bought it here," the male said. "In town."

"As a souvenir, of course," the female quickly added, sidling up to the male. "An *earthling* souvenir, right, dear?" (And did she elbow him in the ribs? Kinda hard? Alien ways of communicating were sometimes a bit odd.) Her blue cheeks were pretty big, and when she smiled they bunched up and squeezed her eyes into slits. "We always like to shop native on vacation and bring a little something home with us."

"Well, you're going to have to put it away," I said.

"We're sorry, it's just that we don't allow photography of any kind," Amy said. "There has been...well, a little trouble with pictures in the past."

I snorted. *A little trouble* was putting it mildly, but Amy was trying to spare my feelings. Last summer a photo of three alien guests had wound up on the front page of the *Forest Grove Gazette,* and it had been my fault.

The blue male's face fell, and he just sort of stared at the phone in his hand. He looked pretty devastated, actually. Part of me felt bad, but this was one rule that I definitely had to enforce. And come on, it was just a picture. He'd get over it.

I was about to say something when the little round female grabbed the phone and tucked it into her purse. "We must do what the young man says, *dear,*" she said, emphasizing the last word the way you do when you're trying to send an unspoken message.

Whatever. As long as the camera was put away and we were all headed back inside for the night, I was good.

"Do we have to keep smiling?" Frog Face said. All of the aliens' strange expressions were frozen hideously in place.

Amy giggled. "No, it's okay. You can relax."

The Tourists' faces went back to "normal" as the group let out a collective sigh of relief. Apparently aliens don't like holding that fakey smile-grimace for the camera any more than humans do.

"You all must be tired," I said. I always got a little messed up by the three-hour time difference after my flight from Florida; I couldn't imagine what jet lag must feel like when you've traveled three million light-years. "Let's get everyone inside."

"Inside? That's a great idea!" the blue male said, clapping his hands in excitement like a little kid. The female gave him another shot to the ribs and he toned it down some. Man, aliens can be weird.

Amy and I led the way down the path. It was one of those rare balmy nights in the Pacific Northwest when it actually felt good to be outside. It wasn't quite like being back home in Tampa, where the night breeze feels almost like warm silk against your skin, but it would do.

An owl hooted at us from his perch on a tree limb, setting

off a hearty chorus of answering *hoo-hoo*s from the aliens. Sometimes they weren't one hundred percent sure which Earth creatures had the power of sophisticated language and which didn't.

The path emptied out on the road, a couple of blocks from the bed-and-breakfast. Grandma's place was pretty isolated from town—the road dead-ended into the forest just past her house—so I wasn't too worried about anyone seeing us.

Amy turned to face the aliens. "Okay, everybody, time to get out your day passes." She shot me a quick *Can-you-believe-my-dad?* expression and then looked back at the Tourists. "Remember, the Head of Security will be checking them at the door when we get back."

It was Tate's latest security measure. In the main room he had set up a bulletin board where he pinned an ID card for every guest. Whenever aliens left the house, they had to take their cards. Upon their return Tate collected the cards and put them back on the board. That way he could tell at a glance who was inside and who was still out.

The aliens rummaged through pockets of the thrift-store clothing they had picked up from Grandma's trunks. Blue Pointy Ears cleared his throat. When he leaned over to Frog Face I heard him ask, "Hey...so what's that card look like again?"

His little mate stepped up to Amy. "I'm afraid we may have misplaced our cards. I'm terribly sorry." She got up on her tiptoes to look over Amy's shoulder, as if trying to get a look at the bed-and-breakfast, but it was around the corner and still out of sight. "I'm sure we'll be allowed back inside anyway, yes?"

"Oh, I'm sure it won't be that big a problem," Amy said. "But you'll definitely have to talk to the Head of Security first."

"Have fun with that," I muttered. "He's not exactly the most approachable guy in the galaxy." Amy whacked me in the arm again, but not too hard. After all, she knew it was true.

I meant it as a harmless joke for Amy, but the female must have heard too—I should have known those pointy ears would have special powers—because her blue face looked really worried all of a sudden. "Hey, I was just kidd—" I started to say, but she was already working her way back through the little crowd, toward her mate.

Amy turned back to the road. "Let's go," she said. "He won't be that hard on them."

We walked along for half a block, but I was feeling guilty. "I shouldn't have freaked her out like that," I told Amy. After a few more steps I said, "I'm going back there to tell her not to worry."

"That's very sweet of you." Amy patted me on the shoulder. "But don't worry, I won't tell anyone that you have a sensitive side. You'll be able to keep your Middle School Boy Membership Card."

"Very funny." I turned and walked to the back of the group . . . but the blue aliens were not there. What the—?

I whipped my head around, scanning the street and the surrounding forest. Having unaccounted-for aliens on the loose was not good.

I retraced our steps, sweeping the flashlight back and forth. Maybe they had stopped to check out an Earth flower, or hoot at some more owls, or whatever. I couldn't imagine why they...

Then I saw something on the ground. It was a few feet off the path, under a fern, right where the underbrush started to get dense.

I bent down and picked it up. It was a rubbery ear, pointy, the kind of thing that you would buy at a *Star Trek* convention to play Vulcan dress-up.

And it had been spray-painted blue.

I looked up again, but the flashlight didn't penetrate more than a few feet into the black forest. They could be anywhere.

I jogged back through the aliens to catch up with Amy. "That blue couple—did you greet them when they arrived?" Amy, Grandma, and I split the duties of welcoming the aliens and checking out their earthling disguises.

"No, I thought *you* did. Or maybe your grandma," she said. "They didn't look familiar, but I figured they had just arrived this evening."

I shook my head and held up the car. Amy's eyes got wide. She took it from me and ran her fingers along its rubbery edge. Then she held up her hand and showed me the faint smudges of blue paint.

"What's going on?" she said. "Why would aliens want to disguise themselves as other aliens?"

"No idea."

Amy chewed on her lower lip. "Unless..."

"Unless what?"

"They aren't aliens. Could they have been people from town? Maybe trying to join in on the big 'alien masquerade party'?"

"Man, I hope not." I felt sick just thinking about it. "I wouldn't want a human to get too close a look at that 'costume' for the alien with that froggy-looking face. It's kind of hard to make a Halloween mask that slobbers and blinks, you know?"

Amy frowned and turned the ear over in her hands. "This doesn't make any sense."

"Like anything around here ever does?"

"Good point." Amy handed the ear back and I shoved it into my pocket. "We'll have to tell my dad, of course. And keep our eyes open for anything strange."

I sighed. "What else is new?"

I saw the lights before I heard the music.

Grandma's place is a strange enough sight to begin with, especially at night. Sure, maybe its jet-black exterior blended in with the forest, but that only emphasized the glow-in-the-dark murals of comets and stars and planets splashed across the entire house. And the silver spaceship structures on the front lawn shone eerily in the moonlight. After dark, the bed-and-breakfast almost looked like outer space itself.

I had gotten used to its appearance by now. But these lights were something new.

Amy and I lurched to a stop at the same time, the crowd

of aliens bumping into us from behind. She made a surprised sound. Or maybe it was me. Our mouths dropped into fly-catching mode as we stared at the house.

Every window was filled with bright, swirling pastels. It looked like someone inside was aiming a dozen spotlights at a giant disco ball for an alien dance party.

But that wasn't even the strangest part. There were... well, I guess you'd have to call them *rainbows*... drifting out from every available opening: windows, the space under the front door, the chimney, even cracks between the shingles. They were long ribbons of multicolored light, but the purples and yellows and oranges and all the rest didn't stay in orderly rows. They melded together to form new combinations or broke apart into dozens of shapes, like bouncing polka dots or squiggly lines that swam about, bringing the patterns to life.

The living rainbows spiraled through the sky, bathing the bed-and-breakfast in a kaleidoscope glow. After two or three passes around the house they would float up into the night to curl around the tops of trees, or coil together into a rainbow whirlpool, or simply rise straight up for the stars, before breaking up like campfire smoke.

It was weird.

After the shock wore off, Amy and I hustled down the street. When we got closer we heard the music. Grandma had one of those antique stereo systems that looks like a big wooden piece of furniture and plays actual records, but I'd never heard it blasting so loud. The song was one of Grandma's old hippie "classics," something about the Age of Aquariums.

Hippie music is weird too.

Then I noticed that the lights were moving in sync with the song. Pulsing in time with the drums; rainbow edges going all jagged when the lead guitar took over, and then smoothing out again with the bass; colors flaring brightly as the singers belted out the chorus.

The group of aliens smiled and nodded along with the music as if nothing was out of the ordinary. Which I guess for them was probably the case. This must have been like coming home.

Amy squinted at the front porch. "Wait—where's my dad?"

Tate wasn't in his usual evening spot, hunched over on the driftwood bench, waiting for the aliens to return. "I don't think he's too interested in collecting day passes right now," I said. "Come on, let's go check it out."

When we opened the front door we saw that, as usual, what was going on inside the B&B was even crazier than how it looked from the outside. Amy and I stopped short and just stared.

It was a psychedelic fever dream come to life. Grandma was twirl-dancing in the middle of the main room in one of her free-flowing, earth-toned tunics. Dozens of bamboo bracelets rattled on her skinny arms as she raised them to the ceiling and waved them in time to the beat. Her face was turned up to take in the swirling lights overhead, her smile beaming even brighter than the rainbows.

She was in hippie heaven.

I finally snapped out of it and pulled Amy inside after me. We ushered in our alien companions, then firmly shut the door. (As if that could possibly help conceal this—whatever *this* was—from the outside world.)

"Who are they?" Amy said, pointing. It was hard to talk over the music, so I just shrugged and lifted both palms: *No idea.*

She was referring to the six aliens circling Grandma. They were long, willowy creatures, with reedy legs that made up more than three-fourths of their overall height. Their torsos were skinny cylinders that sprouted wiry arms almost as long as those legs. They were entirely covered in greenish fuzz, like a tennis ball.

And their heads—each of them had a stretched-out neck that ended in what looked like a big ball of fluff, only with glowing blue eyes and a big smile nestled in the middle.

The group spun around the room, with Grandma in the center. They leaped gracefully over couches and chairs like gymnasts, doing perfect splits in the air, their long legs parallel to the floor. They must not have weighed much; they seemed to float a little with each jump.

When they waved their fuzzy arms around like Grandma was doing, living rainbows wafted up from their fingertips, ribbons of light that rose, whirling, into the air.

Mrs. Crowzen and her students had beat us home, and they were sitting cross-legged around the perimeter of the room, taking in the show, pointing at the rising storm of colors, and chattering away to each other. I think they liked it more than the earthling fireworks show.

Not that I could blame them. The sight was pretty amazing. Hypnotic, even. This was confirmed when I looked over at Amy. Her eyes shone as she took in the scene with the same blissed-out expression as Grandma. Apparently her love of all things alien had won out over the need to protect our big secret. Sometimes I think she must be the one related to Grandma.

I scanned the room for Tate, but he wasn't here. Of course he wasn't here. Tate would be having a heart attack piled on top of a conniption fit wrapped up in a seizure if he was here.

I was going to have to deal with this on my own.

Timing it just right, like I was slipping between converging defenders in a full-court press, I dashed between two of the dancing aliens into the middle of the circle. I took Grandma by the shoulders.

Her eyes went from half-mast to alert behind the wide pink lenses of her glasses. She looked a little startled, like she was waking from a trance. But she didn't miss a beat. Grandma grabbed my arms and pulled me into her twirling.

Great. So now I was technically dancing. Which is something I never do, not even at the middle school dances back home. And definitely not as the center of attention in the middle of an otherworldly light show. With an alien audience. And Amy watching.

"What's going on?" I shouted over the music.

"Oh, isn't this wonderful?" Grandma spread her arms out to indicate the Thin Green Fuzzies circling us. "They've come back at last!"

"Who?"

"The Arkamendian Air Painters!"

As if that explained everything. Or anything.

"Okay, Grandma, but shouldn't—?"

"They are some of my favorite Tourists and they haven't visited in years." More twirling, more beaming.

"But won't they—?"

"They sponsor troupes that travel from planet to planet, interacting with the atmosphere and manipulating the natural surroundings to create these wonderful symphonies of color and light." Her eyes went hazy with joy again as she spun me around.

"Right, but we can't—"

"This is one of their favorite spots because of all the—what is it again?" she called.

"Phosphorescence," several of the dancing aliens said. Even their voices were fuzzy.

"Yes, that's it. Phosphorescence." Grandma sighed dreamily. "They say it makes the colors ever so much brighter. What a glorious spectacle."

All of this spinning was not good. After corn dogs with ketchup and three bottles of orange soda, I was about to make an ever-so-brightly-colored, inglorious spectacle of my own. All over the carpet.

I finally disentangled myself from her grip. "Grandma!" I shouted it pretty loud. She stopped dancing and really looked at me for the first time. "We need to talk."

Grandma went over to the stereo and turned the music down a bit, enough to allow a real conversation. The Air Painters continued to do their thing while the rest of the aliens looked on.

Amy joined us, and we huddled in the corner.

"What is it, David?" Grandma was finally fully present,

studying my face. After what happened at the beginning of summer—not to brag or anything, but I kind of, you know, saved the town and maybe the entire planet or whatever—I think she really trusted me.

"We need to stop this. Right now. You can see it from outside."

Grandma waved away my objections. "Oh, what's a few decorative lights inside a house? Come on, it's a Fourth of July party!"

"Not exactly," Amy said. She explained how the rainbows were flying all over outside.

"Oh, dear." Grandma's face fell. "I usually drive the Air Painters up the mountain and find a nice meadow well away from town." She looked around the sitting room, as if suddenly remembering that her establishment was, indeed, located on planet Earth. "I was just so excited to see them again...."

"Look, I don't think we need to worry too much, Grandma. The whole town was at the park, and they're all walking home now. I'm sure no one is coming this way."

"Yeah," Amy said. "Let's just postpone your little reunion party until tomorrow. We'll even come along, right, David?"

"As long as I don't have to dance." I sort of blurted it out. I felt a little bad, but Grandma didn't seem to notice.

"Okay," she said, sweeping the hair out of her eyes and smoothing her tunic. "I'll just tell everybody to—"

That's when the front door burst open and the Arkamendian Air Painters started screaming.

The thing that zoomed in looked like a purple beach ball with six legs. But when its mouth opened, most of that round body seemed to disappear, and it was more a black cavern with teeth racing into the sitting room.

It took a flying leap onto the couch, bounced off the cushions, and rocketed into the air, jaws snapping furiously in an attempt to "catch" the rainbows. Using the sofa like a trampoline, it wriggled in the air for maximum hang time and tried to bite the colors at the apex of each jump. It made a whistly-growling noise when the rainbows floated out of reach.

The Arkamendian Air Painters broke their circle and dashed all over the room, still screaming fuzzily. The rainbow thingies must have been tied to their emotions or something, because the light-ribbons flashed like neon warning signs and then turned completely black. It looked like an army of shadows swirling around as the room was plunged into a churning gloominess.

This got the bite-happy beach ball even more excited. It leaped off the couch and scampered straight up one of the walls, darting this way and that, big mouth snapping in every direction. Finally, it zoomed above our heads in a circle, body perpendicular to the ground as it clung to the tops of the walls. It moved so fast that it became a purple blur, almost like one of the living rainbows themselves.

The Air Painters huddled together, casting worried glances overhead, their eyes now glowing with an eerie redness that cut through the spinning shadows. Yikes. What had been a bright and beautiful scene a few moments ago had become pretty creepy.

Finally the beach ball creature slowed down, worked its way to the middle of the ceiling and hung there, upside down, mouth gaping wide to collect the ribbons of floating darkness that were drifting upward. A long tongue shot out and whipped around in all directions, apparently trying to lasso the shadow-ribbons and pull them in, frog-style. This did not work.

Grandma put her arms around the Air Painters and spoke in soothing tones as they trembled. Gradually their glowing eyes faded from an alarming red to a softer pink.

But the alien kids were delighted. "Snarffle!" they cried,

laughing and pointing as he kept trying, without any success whatsoever, to eat the rainbows.

All the kids loved Snarffle. He had shown up in one of the short-circuiting transporters at the beginning of summer and now was sort of my pet. And after helping save the planet, he had become the B&B's mascot.

I walked over and stood directly under the purple alien. When he saw me, his little tail whirled in a circle and his tongue wagged so hard that warm slobber drops splattered my face.

I stretched my hands out, palms up. "Come on down, boy." He dropped from the ceiling, straight into my arms. I scratched the pattern of bright blue dots on his backside, and he wriggled all over with pleasure. He still kept one eye on those shadows, though, which were slowly transforming back into tasty-looking rainbows as the Air Painters calmed down.

All of the alien students clapped their little hands when I caught him. (Amy had taught them the human custom of applause, and now they did it whenever they could. I had recently earned clapping for such awesome feats as taking out the garbage and washing the dishes.)

"It's okay," Amy said, joining Grandma in soothing the Arkamendians. Some of them were shivering hard enough to shed green fuzz all over the carpet. (Too bad there aren't vacuum cleaners made for sucking up those hard-to-reach alien fuzz balls.) "Snarffle is our friend. He won't hurt you."

Snarffle dog-smiled and made his happy-whistle to emphasize the point. He twirled his propeller tail even faster, the tip smacking me in the face.

"That's right," Grandma cooed, rubbing the backs of

those willowy aliens. "He just got excited by your beautiful creations. There, there. Nothing to be frightened of."

But what walked through the door next looked more frightening than any slightly crazed, mouth-snapping beach ball from outer space.

Robert Tate's jowly face was brick red, and patches of sweat spread darkly from the armpits of his extra-large khaki uniform. He was fighting to catch his breath, but it came off more like seething. The handle of Snarffle's leash dangled from one white-knuckled fist, ending in shredded material where it must have ripped in half.

The Head of Security kicked the door shut behind him. "Just what"—*huff, gasp*—"in the Sam Hill"—*pant, wheeze*—"is goin' on in here?" Tate stared daggers at the living rainbows still swirling in the air, swiveled his head slowly to take in the alien crowd with a sneer, and leveled a stern gaze at Grandma.

She smiled sweetly at him, then swept both hands grandly at the Arkamendian Air Painters, the gesture completely unapologetic. "Some of my favorite Tourists have returned. We're having a little Welcome Back party."

"But those confounding lights!" He had gotten a little wind back and it came out in a half roar, with some flying spittle for emphasis. The fiery flush of anger spread from his cheeks to his forehead until he almost looked like a Tourist from a demon planet. "I could see 'em three blocks away! And furthermore, I should never have—"

Little Kandeel burst into tears. She was trying to hide behind a lamp stand, and her skin had gone mahogany to match the varnished wood, complete with little knotholes all over her body. I guess some aliens can cry a lot more than humans, because within a few seconds she was standing in a puddle of tears.

Not that I could blame her. If I went to another planet and saw something like Tate, I'd probably start bawling too.

"See what you've done?" Grandma said, hands planted on her hips.

"What *I've* done?" It was a full roar now. "These colors are lighting up the night for everyone to—"

"Oh, hush!" Grandma matched him, volume-wise. "A few lights are one thing, but all of your hot air can't be helping. They can probably hear you in the mayor's office downtown."

Kandeel choked out another sob. Amy moved toward her, but Snarffle was faster. He leaped out of my arms, bounded over to Kandeel, and started licking the tears right off her cheeks. Pretty soon a smile crept across her face, and then she threw both arms as wide as she could and hugged the round alien tight. Her body color morphed into an exact match, right down to the blue polka dots.

Kanduu joined them, first putting an arm around his sister, and then hugging Snarffle along with her. The purple alien quickly switched from sympathetic comforter to shameless affection monger, turning over and angling his patch of bright blue dots toward them so they could scratch his sweet spot. The other students gathered around, laughing, happy to oblige.

I motioned to Amy, and we stepped in between Grandma and Tate, who were still glaring at each other. Sometimes we sort of had to do recess-monitor duty with those two.

"Dad, you can't just come in here yelling and screaming and scaring children," Amy said.

"And Grandma," I added, "you know he has a point. We can't have all of these lights floating around outside."

"May as well put up a neon sign saying 'Aliens on Vacation,'" Tate muttered.

"Oh, why don't you take a twenty-year vacation?" She wouldn't even look at him.

"Really, Grandma?" I tried to use that *I'm-more-disappointed-than-mad* tone that parents are so good at.

"Dad, you're not helping. Let's have a reasonable discussion about this."

Tate cleared his throat. "All righty, I can have a reasonable discussion." He adjusted his belt higher on his round belly. "How about you tell me just what purpose all of this serves?" He gestured above us, where the last traces of rainbow were slipping up the staircase and through the chimney.

"Purpose?" Grandma said. "Oh, isn't that just like you. Sometimes beauty is a purpose in and of itself."

Tate snorted in disgust. "Well, there has to be some reason you'd put the whole operation at risk like this. Any fool could tell something alien is going on here. Any old fool at all." He waved a hand in the air. "From outside, it's like the very sky itself is on fire, swirling around with all of them crazy colors. There's just no other reasonable explanation."

"Well, well . . . that certainly sounds familiar," Grandma said with a mischievous little smile. "I'm sure glad I saved this. Thought it might come in handy someday." She crossed to the coffee table and picked up an old copy of the *Forest Grove Gazette*, the edges of the newspaper yellowed with age. "Remember when you were interviewed after taking your scout troop camping up on the mountain, about five years ago? I took out this article to show the Arkamendians." She held it up so we could see:

SHERIFF GETS RARE GLIMPSE
OF NORTHERN LIGHTS

Local lawman Robert Tate claims to have seen the aurora borealis, the spectacular phenomenon known as the northern lights, from his Mt. Baker–area campsite last Saturday evening.

"It was like the very sky itself was on fire, swirling around with the craziest colors," Sheriff Tate said.

Normally, the natural display of multicolored lights splashed across the sky is only visible from regions much farther north, but Tate insisted this is what he and his Boy Scout troop had witnessed. "There's just no other reasonable explanation," he said. "I may not be much of an astronomer, but any fool could tell you those were the northern lights. Any old fool at all. And besides, it was one of the finest experiences of my life."(*Story continued on page B4*)

Grandma arched one eyebrow playfully as Tate's coloring drained from brick to chalk.

The big man opened his mouth to say something, spluttered, choked, then tried again. His roar had turned into more of a whisper. "You can't mean..."

"I'm afraid I can," Grandma said, waving the newspaper at him. "That was the last time the Air Painters visited." Her grin got even bigger. "In fact, as I snuck past your campsite on the way home, I heard you giving those boys a lengthy lecture on the northern lights. Oh, yes, they got quite an education that night."

Tate looked over at the Arkamendians. They smiled shyly and waved at him, tiny light trails wafting up from their fingers. One of them bowed very low. "It makes us most happy to know that you enjoyed our artwork enough to describe it to the local storytellers." Her voice was fuzzy around the edges, like a radio that's just out of tune. "The whole community learned about it from you. This makes us quite proud."

Tate's face went even paler, if that's possible.

"And we are so grateful for the opportunity to return," another one said. The Air Painters all murmured their thank-yous and gathered around Tate in a tight circle. They started a mini-whirlpool of light, and the colors washed over Tate.

"Oh, my. This is a sign of great honor and respect on their planet," Grandma said. "I think they really like you."

But Tate was just a rainbow-colored lump of grump.

It was Amy who rescued him. She waded through the Air Painters, thanking them for the show, and pulled her dad out of the circle. She sat him on the couch and fetched a glass of water. The fight had gone out of him.

Grandma hugged all of the Fuzzies in a big group. "We'll make sure to go up the mountain soon and put on a heck of a show. We can dance all night!"

The Air Painters drifted upstairs, chattering happily to each other. Tate just slumped on the couch, slowly shaking his head.

I knew that things would need to be put in order before I could go to bed, so I helped Mrs. Crowzen round up her alien students, then collected the day passes from the adult aliens. As I pinned the passes to the board, I remembered the two blue "aliens" we had met earlier tonight. I turned to Tate, ready to tell him about them, but he looked so tired and defeated that I decided it could wait until tomorrow morning. Whoever they were, they took off before they saw all of those crazy rainbows, and it's not like they were knocking the door down or anything.

When just the four of us humans were left, Tate finally lifted his head and snorted out a half-laugh.

"Sometimes I think these two are trying to take over this whole operation," he said to Grandma as he watched Amy and me finish cleaning up.

"I can't imagine anyone who would do a better job." Grandma smiled at us, then leveled her gaze at Tate. The smile disappeared. "Anyone at all."

Amy gave her dad a too-sweet smile, winked at me, then went back to picking green fuzz out of the carpet.

Tate harrumphed and sat up a little straighter. "You're a smart girl, my dear, but there's still a lot you and your friend don't know about all the details that go into keeping a business running smoothly."

I dropped down on one knee beside Amy to help her clean up. "Oh, please," I muttered so only she could hear. "Who does the real work around here half the time, especially when he and Grandma spend so much time arguing?"

"I know," she whispered back. "And remember what he was doing while we were busy trying to save the planet last week?" She made a zoned-out zombie face, an imitation of Tate after he had eaten some tainted alien treats right before the bad guys showed up in their warship.

"What are you two giggling about over there?" Tate demanded.

"Oh, nothing, Dad." Then she whispered to me again. "Just how *impossible* it would be for me and David to keep doing all of our chores without you grumping at us all day."

I rolled my eyes. "How would we even manage to make it out of bed in the morning?" We both hid our laughter behind fake coughs.

Tate shook his head. "There's more to running this place than slapping some used clothing on space creatures, you know. Especially a top secret, high-security operation like this. Believe me, you kids don't know the half of what it takes to keep it all together around here."

Grandma raised one eyebrow. "Who knows? Maybe they'll get their chance someday."

Right. Like that could ever happen.

5

The next morning, I took Snarffle for a walk in the woods before breakfast. *My* breakfast, that is. I had learned from experience that if I didn't feed him right away, he would eat everything in his sight—literally.

Snarffle's "walks" were really not walks at all. He liked to playfully chase woodland creatures, scurry up tree trunks to bounce along the branches, splash through the Nooksack River to cool himself off, and plunge into dense underbrush seeking new plants to eat. Walking Snarffle was like trying to lasso a cyclone.

But occasionally he did have to stop and, you know...

get rid of all that food. And he valued his privacy, suddenly halting that frenetic motion to mince his way daintily behind a cluster of bushes.

So I was leaning against a tree at the edge of the forest, my back to the thicket of underbrush where Snarffle was doing his business, when I saw the hot air balloon.

At first I watched it just because I was curious. You see a few of those around here, but not too many, and it looked pretty cool hanging over the tops of the trees.

But then I squinted and could make out two people leaning over the side of the little basket hanging under the balloon. And they were pointing something at the ground —it was long and black and flared at the end. Maybe a fancy camera with a big zoom lens?

And while I couldn't see the B&B from here, I was suddenly sure that they were hovering right over the house. Taking pictures.

Pictures! My mind flew to the last time someone had tried to take a picture around here. I thrust my hand into my pocket, and there was the rubber ear. (Okay, maybe Amy was right about me not exactly changing my clothes every single day in the summer.) I pulled out the ear and examined it, cursing myself for not showing it to Tate and Grandma last night.

Snarffle finally finished, and for a change I dragged *him,* in my haste to get back. By the time we had made it through the forest and returned to the house, the balloon had drifted away, over the town. I relaxed a little bit—it was probably just a couple of random sightseers—but I was still going to have to mention it to Grandma and Tate, and tell them about the blue ear.

When we got inside, a group of Tourists was sitting around the big communal table in the kitchen. The Air Painters were there, as well as a few brightly colored families and individual Tourists that I recognized from the fireworks outing. As soon as we entered, they all hunched over their plates protectively. Apparently Snarffle's reputation preceded him.

But Grandma was prepared, as always. Humming one of her hippie songs, she pulled a cookie sheet out of the oven. It was piled high with a towering stack of wheat-germ pancakes, a dozen baked apples, three loaves of organic banana-nut bread, and a mixing bowl full of oatmeal and molasses. "Here you go, sweetie. I kept it warm for you."

"Thanks, Grandma," I said. "I'm starv—"

Before I realized that the food wasn't intended for me, and before Grandma even had time to set it down on the floor, Snarffle was inhaling it all, tail twirling like a fan.

Tate grumbled to no one in particular from behind his newspaper. "That thing is fixing to eat up every penny of the profits around here."

Oh, please. As if someone Tate's size should be complaining about the grocery bill. But I guess I should cut him a little slack—after all, he was sort of semiconscious and zombified when Snarffle helped us save the world earlier in the summer, so he didn't know that the little guy was more than your average space pet.

"Hey, Grandma. Can I talk to you about something?" I inclined my head toward the door, indicating the need for privacy. I didn't want to tell Tate until I talked to Grandma first, see if she knew anything about the blue ear—maybe she had given them out as novelty door prizes or something, who knows? Tate's first tendency was to overreact.

"Of course, dear, just give me a few minutes to finish up."

I nodded and sat down, trying to find something to eat that wasn't too insanely healthy. But just then Amy poked her head in through the swinging door, glanced over her shoulder, and stepped halfway in. She seemed hesitant and uncertain. It was very un-Amy-like.

Grandma looked up from the stove. "Yes, dear?"

"A group of aliens just showed up to see you...." Amy swallowed. "Only I don't think they're interested in a place to stay."

Tate put down his paper, revealing a frown, and got up to move toward Amy in the doorway. Grandma straightened up and wiped her hands on a dish towel. "Yes? Well, show them in."

Amy pushed the door open, and a gaggle of aliens bustled right past her and her dad. They were about three feet high and squarish, like smaller versions of a roadside mailbox. Instead of arms they had a swarm of snakelike growths sticking out from their bodies, each one ending in a different shape: knob, net, bulb, vise grip. The Swiss Army knife of alien appendages.

Oh, and each alien balanced on a single sturdy block of a leg. There was lots of hopping.

I shot a glance at Amy, but she just lifted her eyebrows and shrugged: *Who knows?*

"What's all this about?" Tate said.

Grandma waved him off. "May I help you?" she said.

But the Hopping Mailboxes didn't pay either of them much attention. They were very businesslike, bouncing around the room in tight formation. Clearly the group had some sort of mission, but I couldn't tell what it was.

One of them stood in the middle of the kitchen, two long feelers extended and waving in the air, and hopped around in a little circle as if he was surveying the area. Then he gestured to a couple of the others. In response, one of them nestled into the far corner and aimed a few appendages at the kitchen door. Suddenly, white light flashed out from the tips, and a bright light framed the entrance. The other alien set up camp by the stove and did the same thing, and Grandma was caught in the middle of the spotlight, squinting into the glare.

Two other Mailboxes moved to opposite sides of the room, backs pressed up against the wall. A single feeler from each one extended and snaked straight up, angled at the top of the wall to run along the ceiling, then dropped down to dangle in the air, one right above Grandma and one over the door.

Tate tugged on his mustache and his frown lines deepened. "You ever seen anything like this?" he muttered. Grandma and Amy just shook their heads and watched.

Tate uncrossed his arms and leaned forward; I could tell he was getting ready to lumber into action the moment things went sideways.

He was always overprotective, but in this instance it seemed like a good idea. I had already learned that while most aliens are great, not all of them are friendly. Or peaceful. I looked around for a potential weapon . . . and came up with a butter knife. Covered in syrup. Oh well, it was better than nothing. If these aliens were dangerous, there was always a chance they were deathly allergic to Mrs. Butterworth's.

I snapped my fingers close to the ground, and Snarffle hurried over to stand guard by my side, eyeing this new group warily.

The next two Mailboxes to enter were taller but leaner. One pointed all of its feelers at the door, while the other focused on Grandma.

I tried to gauge the possible danger level by the reaction of the Tourists around the table. They definitely seemed more excited than afraid, whispering to each other and pointing at the workmanlike crew of aliens. In fact, one of them—a big Tourist whose head looked like it was made of cottage cheese —was waving frantically at the newly arrived Mailboxes, a goofy grin spread across his lumpy face.

I studied the scene for a moment. The lights, the things dangling from the ceiling, the oversize boxes pointed at Grandma . . . it was familiar, in a way. It all sort of looked like—

"What in tarnation?" Tate said. "It looks like you're setting up a durn movie set right in the kitchen."

"Quiet, please," said one of the square aliens, adjusting his feelers.

"You don't tell me to be quiet in my—"

Another Mailbox nudged open the kitchen door and peeked his head in. "Ready for him?" he asked the others in clipped tones.

"Action!" called one of the boxy spotlighters.

Amy and Grandma—ever trusting—were excited to find

out more about whatever was going on. Tate looked ready to toss everyone right out the door like a bouncer.

The last Mailbox hopped the rest of the way in and held the door open with his body. Then he waved a few of his snaky appendages rhythmically in front of him, kind of like a maestro leading an orchestra, and music blared out from the tips. Loud music with lots of crashing and blaring, but nothing sinister. More like the prelude to some big event.

And then the Big Event himself made his grand entrance, striding through the doorway in time to the music, wearing a three-legged suit that looked like it was made entirely of white spandex and sequins. He stopped in the exact center of the spotlight, spread out his arms and— Wait, do they really do *jazz hands* in outer space?

Apparently so. And you know how some guys use a bunch of grease to slick their hair back so it looks kinda wet and shiny all day, and seems like it's always being blown backward even when there isn't any wind? Well, this alien looked like that all over, anywhere that wasn't covered by his suit. All sleek and glistening and windswept. He seemed to be in constant motion, even when he just stood there gazing at the oversize Mailboxes.

The triumphant music swelled to a crescendo and then dropped off, replaced by soft, tinkling notes. The sleek alien turned his attention to Grandma and gave her a dazzling smile. Literally dazzling. His teeth reflected the spotlight so much that they were hard to look at directly.

"Are you the proprietor of the Intergalactic Bed and Breakfast, located here on Earth in the Milky Way Galaxy?"

His voice was deep and smooth, like a guy announcing prize packages on a game show.

Grandma nodded slowly, glancing around at the surrounding Mailboxes. It was pretty unsettling to see her speechless.

"Congratulations!" The slick alien sidled up next to Grandma and threw an arm around her shoulders. He sort of bumped her sideways so he was in the exact center of the spotlight.

Tate lurched forward. "You can't come in here and start grabbing—"

"Dad, that guy doesn't exactly look dangerous." Amy took her father's arm and gestured at the alien's sparkly clothes.

"Indeed." The new alien flashed another smile at one of those taller box-aliens, teeth sparkling away. "Ladies and gentlemen and hybrids, I present to you this year's grand prize winner!"

Mr. Slick beamed at Grandma, but she just stood there, looking around in confusion.

"Don't be shy now; this is your shining moment. Give a big Earth hello to the adoring crowd back at the convention!" His arm swept with a flourish toward the two tall aliens.

Grandma's eyebrows crinkled up. "Hello?"

"Hold it a minute." Tate shook off Amy's grip. "Just who is she supposed to be talking to? And what's this convention you're going on about?"

Mr. Slick made a quick head gesture at the Mailbox who had been directing traffic. The little alien hopped over to Tate and whispered, "Please, sir. Be seated and remain quiet. We are in the middle of a live broadcast."

Tate was apparently so surprised that he did exactly as he was told, slumping into the chair next to me. But I heard him mutter, "Just who does he think he is?"

The frog-faced Tourist, seated next to Tate, gaped at the Head of Security, his wet lips pulled into an astonished circle. "You mean you've never heard of Evanblatt Snappyfalls?" he whispered.

Cottage Cheese Head looked over. "I thought everyone in the universe knew the name Evanblatt Snappyfalls."

Frog Face nodded. "He hosts all the big award shows." He looked at Tate's bewildered expression and added, "You know...the Squigglies? And the Moojies? Why, he even hosts the—"

Tate snorted. "Good gravy, there's aliens that are *famous*?"

"Quiet, please," the Mailbox said.

Evanblatt Snappyfalls did that TV maneuver where he leaned in as if he were letting Grandma in on a little secret, but still spoke in his announcer's voice, loud enough for us all to hear. "At this point you've probably guessed why we've come all the way here, am I right?" He nudged Grandma with his elbow. "Or am I right?"

He was wrong. Grandma knew a ton about aliens, but I could tell by the helpless look on her face that she was just as confused as the rest of us. Us humans, at least. Cottage Cheese Head and his alien pals around the table looked about ready to burst with otherworldly joy.

Grandma blinked a few times. "Well, I can't imagine why you—"

"That's right!" boomed Snappyfalls, gazing straight at the

taller Mailboxes. "You've won the Intergalactic Hotelier of the Year Award!"

Amy let out a little gasp as the aliens banged their elbows on the table, hooted like owls, and waved their silverware in the air in celebration (apparently she hadn't taught these Tourists how to applaud yet).

"Is that so?" Grandma grinned, finally looking like herself again. "Well, that certainly sounds like quite the honor. And thank you so much for coming by to tell me. But if you don't mind, I need to finish up with the breakfast dishes, and then I need to clean out the—"

Snappyfalls boomed out a fake announcer's laugh. "Oh no, no, no, my dear. I'm afraid you don't understand. You need to come along with me. We can't disappoint all of those conventioneers by denying them an appearance by the guest of honor!"

"Whatever do you mean?"

"The Hoteliers Association is holding its grand meeting. And they need to see you in the flesh, my dear."

Grandma placed a palm on her chest. "You mean you're asking me to...?" The oversize lenses of her pink glasses made her surprised eyes look huge, and it was easy to see the light of recognition turning on in her head. "The transporters...? You actually want *me* to go through one of the...?"

If Snappyfalls's smile got any bigger, his lips were going to meet in the back of his head and the whole thing might fall right off his neck. "Yes! We're taking you on an all-expenses-paid trip to Callabans!"

Tate stood up, his belly banging against the table. "You're

not taking her anywhere," he said, but was drowned out by the reaction of the aliens.

"Callabans!" Frog Face nodded enthusiastically. "I've been dying to go, but it's so expensive."

Cottage Cheese Head squealed and leaned over to tell me, "They call Callabans the Planet of Perpetual Celebration, you know."

The Arkamendian Air Painters chattered in their fuzzy voices. "The atmosphere there is perfect for our creations! Remember how bright the colors were?"

A few of them started waving their hands around, lost in remembrance, and some rainbows drifted up until Tate stood on the chair and waved them all away with his hand. "None of that, ladies," he growled.

Snappyfalls finally broke his stare at the tall "camera" Mailboxes and saw Grandma's expression, a mixture of confusion, excitement, fear, and wonder.

"Don't worry," he said. "We'll have you right back here before Callabans has time to make a full revolution around its triplet tropical suns." He directed his smile at the Tourists around the table. "Why, they'll hardly know you're gone."

6

Grandma looked around at us humans, a question in her eyes.

Tate crossed his meaty arms over his chest, frowning and shaking his head slowly.

Amy was equally easy to read. She was bouncing up and down and doing little air claps, as if Christmas, her birthday, and the start of summer vacation were all happening on the same day.

Grandma looked at me last, and I guess I wasn't sure how I felt about it. I mean, it would be really weird if she wasn't here, right? I knew she'd probably have fun, but Grandma was the only one who ever—

"Right this way, my dear." Snappyfalls took her by the elbow and led her toward the door.

"Wait a moment." Grandma slipped her arm out of his and smoothed her long hair into place. "This is all quite flattering, but I'm afraid I can't leave. There's simply too much to be done around here."

"Spoken like a true Intergalactic Hotelier of the Year," Snappyfalls said, pretend-chuckling at his own little joke. "I think it's time to introduce you to the folks who are eagerly awaiting your arrival."

He nodded at one of the taller Mailboxes, then swept his hand toward the far kitchen wall with a flourish. The Mailboxes aimed their feelers, and light came streaming out in a thin beam like a projector. The wall instantly became a screen.

Only it was so much better than a screen. It was as if the entire wall had disappeared, and we were peering directly into a cavernous auditorium filled with hundreds of aliens of every color and shape imaginable. With antigravity streamers floating overhead and the crowd decked out in flamboyantly silly outfits, the whole place was so fancy that it didn't seem real. Kind of like an awards show on Earth, I guess.

When all of the aliens waved at us and cheered, it made my parents' high-def, 3-D entertainment system with surround sound look like an ancient black-and-white job. I don't know if it was holograms or what, but it seemed like I could step right into that auditorium and touch those aliens. (Man, I wish Earth would hurry up on the technology development.

How cool would it be to watch the NBA playoffs like you were sitting right in the middle of the court?)

I just stared, but Tate rushed over and placed himself in front of Grandma, blocking her from the wall screen. The Head of Security put his hands on his hips, standing guard, as though the well-dressed aliens were going to start an invasion of the planet in our kitchen and applaud all the earthlings to death.

Snappyfalls ignored him. "These are your peers, my good woman. Intergalactic innkeepers from every reach of the cosmos," he said. "They have voted for you to receive their most prestigious award and are now waiting to congratulate you in the flesh."

Grandma peeked out from behind Tate's shoulder at all of those aliens. She reached up with one hand and gave a tentative little wave. The crowd went wild, cheering so loudly that the coffee cups shook on our table.

Tate winced and clamped his hands over his ears. "You're not going anywhere. You can't!" he shouted over the noise. "You just can't."

When the cheering died down, Amy rushed over to Grandma, unable to control herself any longer. "Oh, you have to go. You just have to!" It looked like she was in a smiling contest with Evanblatt Snappyfalls.

"Do . . . do you really think so?" Grandma said.

"Just think about it—you won't have to hide anything at all while you're there! You're forced to waste so much of your time keeping all of this a secret. If you went off-world, you could just relax and enjoy everything. Oh, it would be the best time ever!" Amy sighed and got a faraway look in her eyes. "In fact, if it's okay . . . I mean, if you don't mind . . . maybe you could even ask if you could take—"

"You're not going anywhere, young lady," Tate said.

Amy crossed her arms over her chest and glared. She was almost as good at it as her dad. *"Fine."* She spat the word. "But you have no right to keep her from going."

Snappyfalls wedged himself into the middle of the little scrum. "Before you decide"—he waggled his slick triple layer of eyebrows and paused dramatically—"perhaps you would like to say hello to one of your former guests. After all, he is the one who nominated you for this award."

He gestured to the wall screen. An alien in the front row of the auditorium stood up. He was very tall, impossibly thin, and still wearing the fedora and shabby suit from Grandma's trunk of used clothes.

"Mr. Harnox!" Amy and I spoke at the same time, waving at him. He was the first alien I had ever met around here. (Or, you know, anywhere.)

He smiled and waved back. Then he cupped his long gray fingers around his mouth and shouted, "Please to come and say the hello. Such good time we will be having!"

Grandma blew him a kiss. This was met with confused looks from the alien audience. I guess that gesture would look pretty weird if you'd never seen it before.

"Mr. Harnox wrote the most glowing review of you and this establishment and sent it to the nomination committee," Snappyfalls said. "And he's quite right, you know; there will be good times. Very good times, indeed. An event like this is a great opportunity to talk shop and compare notes with hoteliers from all over the universe."

Grandma looked up at the ceiling, thinking things over. Snappyfalls pressed on. "And don't forget the big Intergalactic Social, all of the great food, and the guided tours of the most fun planet in three galaxies. . . . Need I say more?"

Grandma turned to me. "Well, what do you think, David?"

It was a really good question. I know this might sound stupid, but I had always been so busy dealing with what came *out* of the transporters that I had not given much thought to going *into* one of them.

It would be hard to have her gone. Totally. Because Tate would be in charge, and that's definitely not something that sounded like very much fun. For anyone.

But it's like Amy and I were talking about last night—we totally had things covered around here.

And as I really thought about Grandma, I realized she had spent almost her whole life being the only human on the planet to hear firsthand accounts of the wonders of a thousand different galaxies . . . and yet she had always been stuck here in this house. It would kinda be like watching basketball from the bleachers but never getting to go out and actually play in a game. Only, you know, way worse, since we're talking about the entire universe here. That would stink.

"I think you should go," I said. "You deserve it. Besides, he said it would only be for a little while, right? Just long enough for the planet to do something with its three suns?"

Cottage Cheese Head nodded, his lumpy white face quivering. "That's only about a week in Earth terms."

Tate groaned. "A whole week?"

Grandma got a little fidgety with her hands. "That *is* kind of a long time to be away. . . ."

"But you can't possibly pass up an opportunity like this!" Amy blurted out.

"Yeah, Grandma, a week will fly by around here like nothing ever happened." I shrugged. "I think we can manage to keep the b-and-b from floating away into the atmosphere for seven days or so."

Grandma looked at me. "You only get to come out on your summer vacation, David. I hate to leave while you're here."

"There's over a month of summer left. We can still hang out when you get back. You should go. Really."

Grandma leaned in and kissed my cheek. "Thank you, dear." She straightened up, took off her apron, and draped it over the back of a kitchen chair. "Yes," she said, looking up at Snappyfalls. "I'll go with you."

The alien audience went crazy again. Their reaction startled me—I was so focused on Grandma that I had forgotten about the wall screen for a minute. Getting used to stuff like that so easily was the weirdest part about working at the Intergalactic Bed & Breakfast. I mean, being on a TV broadcast for aliens in a distant galaxy was only the third or fourth strangest thing to happen to me this week.

Grandma took a deep breath, and when she exhaled she looked more like herself: happy and hopeful. "I suppose I should pack a bag if I'm going on a trip."

"Oh, no, my dear, everything will be provided for the guest of honor." Snappyfalls put his arm around Grandma and led her away from us. "The finest clothing, the choicest foods—the bounty of the cosmos will be yours to..." His voice trailed off as they exited the room.

We were all silent for a few moments, taking in what had

just happened. A hush fell over the auditorium aliens too, as they watched and waited.

Tate shifted uneasily, crossing and uncrossing his arms, and tugging at his mustache. He couldn't decide where to direct his glare: at the empty kitchen doorway, or at the auditorium, or at the Mailboxes. Finally he settled on Amy and me. "I can't believe you two would..." he spluttered, shaking his head and looking away. "I mean, it's just not possible that..." He threw his hands up in disgust. "Don't look at me, because I certainly won't be the one who tries to..."

Then he dashed past the stove and out the kitchen door. When Tate was motivated, he could move his bulky frame with astonishing speed.

"He's going to try and stop her," I said to Amy.

"I know." Was she smiling a little bit?

"Are you going to try to talk him out of it?"

"No."

"Why not?"

"I think it's sort of cute that he's so worried about her."

"Worried about *her*?" I gestured to the Tourists sitting around the kitchen table and whispered, "He just doesn't want to be here alone for a week, in charge of them."

Amy sighed and shook her head. "Boys don't understand anything."

Whatever. "I wonder if he'll be able to get to her in time for—"

I was cut off by the wildest ovation yet from the distant crowd of aliens.

Tate was too late—Grandma had already been transported to Callabans! We watched the kitchen wall as she walked out in front of the raucous crowd, waving and blowing kisses to the audience. Evanblatt Snappyfalls paraded her to the center of the stage. It seemed like the entire universe was cheering for her.

She stepped down into the audience, in front of Mr. Harnox. He extended his long gray arms, and she got lost inside his hug. Snappyfalls motioned to the Mailboxes in the auditorium, and the triumphant music started up again. The Tourists around our kitchen table started up a cheer of their own, and the Air Painters whipped up a mini rainbow-tornado.

Grandma stepped out of Mr. Harnox's embrace, turned, and looked right at us. There were tears leaking out of the corners of her eyes (seriously, the high-def on this screen was amazing), but I don't think I'd ever seen her so happy.

Snarffle started up a confused whistle-whining. He looked back and forth from Grandma's usual spot at the stove to where she was standing in the auditorium. When Grandma lifted her hand to wave at us, Snarffle took a running leap at her . . . and crashed face-first into the wall. He grunted in surprise and scampered back to us, whimpering.

Amy dropped down and put her arm around him, scratching at his blue dots. "It's okay, boy," she said. "She's going to be just fine."

When I lifted my hand to wave back, the auditorium and all of its aliens suddenly disappeared, leaving a blank kitchen wall.

The Mailboxes turned off their lights and sucked those snaky appendages back into their bodies with a slurpy hiss.

Then they hopped single file out the door. No more music, no more screen. No more Grandma.

For the first time in forty years, she was not in charge of the Intergalactic Bed & Breakfast.

7

"Attention! I need every vision sensor or antenna or whatever-you've-got focused on me, understand? There're going to be a few changes around here." Tate pulled a slip of paper out of his shirt pocket and waved it around. "Maybe more than a few."

He marched back and forth in front of the Tourists assembled in the main room, a drill sergeant addressing new recruits. Grandma had barely been gone an hour and here he was, already establishing his new regime.

Tate unfolded the paper. "Rule Number One: No leaving

the premises in groups larger than three. Attracts too much attention."

"Excuse me?" Mrs. Crowzen, seated in the middle of the couch and surrounded by her students, clacked her claws together nervously. "That will eliminate all field trip opportunities. I have promised the children's parents that I will provide the best—"

"Rule Number Two: No discussion of the new rules." Tate leveled his gaze at her, waiting for a challenge that didn't come, and then resumed his pacing. "Rule Number Three: No leaving the premises between sunset and dawn."

The Arkamendian Air Painters, huddled together in the corner, buzzed with indignation. "But that is the ideal time for our creations. A night sky, softly illuminated by only moonlight and starshine, is the best backdrop for—"

Tate snorted. "There's an old adage in law enforcement, ladies: *Nothing good happens after dark.* It's my intention to eliminate problems before they even start. Ounce of prevention and all that."

"But just look at this." One of the Air Painters stirred her hands in the air until a pale, see-through rainbow appeared. "In full daylight, the beauty of our creations is so diminished that it hardly—"

"No, no, no!" Tate rushed at the light-ribbon, but it floated above his head. He clambered up onto the arm of the couch and batted the air all around the rainbow, breaking it up like smoke. He huffed and wheezed and almost lost his balance. It might have been funny if the whole situation wasn't so messed up.

When the light had fully dissipated, Tate dropped back to the floor and picked up his rule sheet again, smoothing it out against his chest.

The Air Painters shook their fluffy heads, green fuzz fluttering to the ground, but they remained silent.

"Rule Number Four: No more unhygienic messes all over the house. Too many deep-space germs and microbes and who-knows-what are being spread around here." He pointed a thick finger at the slime-dripping boys, who were sitting in front of the couch, their yellowish-green puddles of goop spreading out on the surrounding floorboards. "That means you two don't leave your rooms—for the rest of your stay here."

"Dad!" Amy jumped out of her chair, hands on hips. "They came from millions of light-years away to observe our planet."

Tate shrugged. "Every guest room comes equipped with a genuine see-through glass window. Great for observing all manner of things." Before Amy could say anything else, her dad turned and jerked his head at Snarffle. "Same goes for him. That thing doesn't leave the house, David."

Now it was my turn to protest. "What? Seriously? With his level of energy? In two days he'll burn holes right through the walls with all of his racing around."

"It's your job to see that he don't."

"But how am I supposed to—"

"Was there something about Rule Number Two that you didn't understand, boy?" Tate took a step toward me and puffed out his chest.

I slumped back in my chair, and Snarffle whistle-growled deep in his throat beside me. There was really nothing we could do except lie low and wait for Grandma to get back.

Tate continued his pacing and reading. No more of this. No more of that. All trips to town had to be chaperoned by a human and take place between the ungodly hours of six and seven thirty a.m. (before Forest Grove's "rush hour," I guess). Then he said something about a firm lights-out time every evening. To be honest, after Rule Number Twenty-three I sort of zoned out.

As my eyes drifted around the room, I noticed that the bricks in the fireplace were shaking. Were we having an earthquake?

Then I realized only a small patch of bricks was moving. It was Kandeel, once again blending in perfectly with the background. Except she was shivering all over as she cringed on the mantel. Poor thing. Tate must have been terrifying to her.

What would she tell her parents about earthlings when she went back to her home planet? She'd probably grow up to write scary stories about grumpy, shouting, big-bellied creatures that could bore you to death with their lists of stupid rules.

I eased out of my seat and slid over to maybe, I don't know, try to comfort her or whatever, but Kanduu beat me to it. He leaned across his little sister and whispered to me, "Is he from a skin-changing planet, like us?"

I shook my head a little when Tate looked the other way. "No, he's native. Why?"

"His face turns so red when he yells, it looks like some kind of camouflage or warning system or something."

"Tell me about it."

Tate droned on. All around me the aliens were drooping.

They stared at the floor, shoulders slumped (the ones who had shoulders, at least), softly murmuring to themselves. It looked like a locker room after a big loss. Something told me that Tate was never going to be nominated for the Intergalactic Hotelier of the Year award.

Finally, the big man folded up his rule sheet and tucked it back into his pocket. "Aside from these minor additions to the house rules, everything will proceed as normal."

"*Minor additions?*" Amy said. "Just what is left for them to do—sit on the front porch and watch the grass grow?"

Tate shook his head. "Weren't you listening? Rule Number Seventeen: No sitting on the front porch."

"But we definitely still get to watch the grass grow, right?" said a roundish blob of a pink alien sprawled across the love seat. "Please tell me I didn't cross three galaxies only to miss out on that." It was sort of refreshing to see that sarcasm extended past Earth's atmosphere.

"That is correct." Unfortunately, Tate didn't really do irony. "As long as you're watching it in the backyard at an approved time." When the Blob rolled his eyes, they made two full revolutions around his sockets.

Tate surveyed the room. "Any more questions?"

Amy was seething, arms folded across her chest, clearly too upset to trust herself to open her mouth.

I figured I should at least try. "You realize that my grandma's not going to like any of this, right?"

Tate harrumphed. "Well, she shouldn't have run off with Slappypants or Sloppyface or whatever his name was."

"But it was the chance of a lifetime!" Amy blurted out.

"Then I hope she's enjoying it."

The aliens were all so slumped over in defeat they looked like they were from planets where bones had never evolved. Thinking of how upset that would make Grandma gave me a shot of courage.

I stood up. "Do you even realize how much Amy and I do around here already? We can pick up the slack until Grandma gets back. Nothing has to change for the Tourists." I glanced at Amy, encouraged by the look of renewed hope in her eyes. "We can handle it. I know we can."

Tate was still for a long time. His voice was quiet when he finally spoke, which was somehow worse than all of his gruff bluster. "So, you think you can handle it?"

I nodded.

"Just like you handled getting a picture of those aliens on the front page of the newspaper last summer? And how you handled getting all of those TV cameras up here last week when you froze the entire river from Mount Baker all the way to Bellingham Bay?"

I sat back down. What could I say to that? But I still knew that we could do it.

"Anything else you want to handle?"

I shook my head.

Tate clapped his hands once, then rubbed them together. "Anyone else ... questions? No? Good." He glanced at his watch. "Everyone is required to meet back here at eighteen hundred hours for a predinner meeting and check-in. If anyone needs me, I will be sweeping the perimeter of the grounds and securing the building." He stopped at the front door and addressed the crowd one more time. "Goes without saying, I'm sure, but anyone caught breaking a rule will be sent home immediately."

"Do you promise?" said the Pink Blob.

But nobody was laughing.

The rest of the day was pretty brutal.

Amy tried to make forced quarantine as fun as possible for the Tourists. At lunchtime she made an elaborate meal for a picnic in the backyard (acceptable to Tate if held between noon and twelve forty-five and the noise level remained below fifty-five decibels, according to Rule Number Forty-two). In the evening she gathered everyone in the sitting room for something she called Earth's Greatest Stories, and she read aloud from Grandma's collection of classics. The aliens thought our sci-fi was pretty cheesy, of course, so she hit them with stories like "The Emperor's New Clothes" as well as stuff with more action, like King Arthur, and the *Grimm's Fairy Tales* (Kanduu and his friends liked all of the blood and gore in those).

But it just wasn't enough to make up for all the lame new rules. In less than twenty-four hours, almost all the guests had cut their vacations short and cleared out of the bed-and-breakfast. Newly arriving Tourists must have been warned by the others, because they opted to hop back into the transporters immediately, maybe trying to salvage a last-minute vacation somewhere else.

And I suspect that's exactly the way Tate wanted it.

Earlier in the summer he had built a combination fire escape/watchtower on the side of the house, and he spent most of the day sitting up top, like a prison warden keeping a sharp eye on the grounds. He always had a pair of binoculars with him, and if he spied anyone from town coming down our road—even just a lone jogger or a mom pushing a baby stroller—he leaned his head inside the window and blew twice on this really loud whistle. The aliens were supposed to go hide in their rooms until he deemed the coast was clear (which he indicated by blowing four times on that stupid whistle).

He only climbed down from his tower long enough to install security cameras on each corner of the house. I don't know how long he'd had them in storage, just waiting to mount them up there like black mechanical gargoyles watching every movement, but I do know that Grandma would never have allowed it.

My guess was they were just for show, to make anybody prowling around think twice. In fact, the cameras probably weren't even hooked up—I'd be surprised if Tate actually knew anything about electronics. But they were big and clunky and obvious, so maybe they would work to scare someone off. Just like Tate seemed to be scaring off most of our business.

By the second day of his reign, the house was pretty much empty except for Mrs. Crowzen and her class on the second floor, and the Arkamendian Air Painters on the third. On the fourth floor there were only Cottage Cheese Head and the Pink Blob (which, by the way, would be a pretty cool name for a rock band).

I had to do something soon, or else Grandma was going to come back to an empty house. And if word got out about how boring the place had become, who knew how long it would take before it filled up again?

But . . . well, it was kind of her fault. I mean, it was hard not to be annoyed that Grandma hadn't trusted Amy and me with more responsibilities when she left. After all the work we'd done around here, it wasn't like we were your typical middle schoolers with a summer job like babysitting or picking berries. And she had to know how messed up everything would get with Tate in charge.

She just left him the keys to the place because he's a grown-up. And that's . . . what do you call it? Ageism. That's what it is. Blatant ageism.

I knew that Amy and I could run this place all by ourselves way better than Tate ever could.

· ◈ ·

"Yee-ha?" Kanduu said, running his fingers along the brim of the white cowboy hat. "Is that the correct pronunciation of this earthling interjection? *Yee-ha?* It sounds kind of silly."

"Well, you might be, like, overthinking it a little. It's not really a word, just sort of a noise you're supposed to let loose while you're riding." I grabbed the hat and whipped it around over my head. "Yeeeee-haw!" I tossed the hat back. "Like that."

"Okay...and that's supposed to help somehow?"

"I guess. That's how all the cowboys do it."

"Hmmmmm." Kanduu put the hat back on, and his head instantly turned white to match. "Isn't riding an Earth cow pretty easy, though? The ones Amy showed us looked very tame. They hardly moved at all."

"What? No. Cowboys don't ride cows. They ride horses."

"Then why don't they call them horseboys? Earthlings are weird."

"Yeah, you've mentioned that a time or two. Look, do you want to do this or not?"

Kanduu looked at Snarffle, who was panting heavily and bouncing up and down in anticipation. All his pent-up energy from being cooped up in the house gave him a crazed expression. More crazed than usual, I should say.

Kanduu tiptoed over and reached out to test the makeshift saddle—a couch cushion strapped on with bungee cords—perched snugly on top of Snarffle's back.

"So it's on there pretty tight?" he said.

"Totally."

Kanduu nodded, studying Snarffle and his saddle, but he still didn't get on.

"Hurry up!" said one of the slime-drippers. "David, if he doesn't go, it's my turn next."

"No way, it's mine," said another little guy, the one with the leathery reptile skin.

The four boy aliens were bouncing almost as much as Snarffle in their excitement to get started.

It had been Amy's idea to split up for the afternoon—her taking the girls, and me with the boys—to try to entertain the kids while Mrs. Crowzen took a well-deserved nap.

I had no idea what Amy's plans were, but my goal was to think of something that I would have found really fun when I was little. It's hard to come up with a cool, rambunctious activity when you're stuck inside the house.

But I did: Snarffle Rodeo.

"Are you ready, bud?" I asked Kanduu. "Or should we give someone else the first crack at it?"

He still wasn't too sure. But then Snarffle gave him a big lick across the cheek (Kanduu's face briefly flaring purple with the contact) and a goofy dog-smile. Kanduu nodded. "I'm ready."

Kanduu jumped onto Snarffle's back, his body turning brown to match the saddle. I handed him the bungee reins, started the stopwatch function on my phone, then gave Snarffle a light smack across his pattern of blue dots.

That purple beach-ball body launched forward at laser speed. Snarffle did a half dozen blurry revolutions around the room before scampering up the wall. He clung to the walls, circling over the heads of the cheering boy aliens, before doing figure eights across the ceiling.

Kanduu threw his head back and laughed, and even managed to hold on with one hand while the other whipped his hat around in the air. "Haw-yeeeeee-HOO!"

"That's close enough," I shouted. "Ride 'em, horseboy!"

Snarffle leaped from the ceiling to the back of the couch. His body tilted on impact as his feet tried to grip the narrow landing strip of furniture, and Kanduu was thrown off. He crashed softly, sinking into all of the throw pillows and winter coats we had put on the floor for padding.

Kanduu popped back up. "That was better than a bag full of krakklefrax!" he said, beaming as his classmates cheered for him.

I looked at the stopwatch. "Thirty-two seconds," I announced.

"Is that good?"

"Good? Professional rodeo guys who ride the bucking broncos aim for eight seconds, and those things are nowhere near as wild as Snarffle," I told him. "It's better than good. It's a universe-wide record." Kanduu waved the hat over his head triumphantly. I looked over at the rest of the boys. "Thirty-two seconds is the time to beat. Who wants to try?"

There was a blur of colors and scales and flying specks of slime as all the boy aliens waved their appendages in the air. I pointed to the reptilian kid. "You're up." The rest of them groaned as the gray, leather-skinned boy raced over to Snarffle and climbed up into the saddle. I strapped him in, making sure to—

"What's going on? I thought we were having an earthquake, the way the whole house was shaking." Amy stood in the doorway, scanning the room. It probably looked like burglars had just ransacked the place. "What are you guys doing?"

"Oh, you know, just hanging out."

"What's that on Snarffle's back?"

The purple alien's long tongue wagged at the mention of his name, splattering slobber drops everywhere.

"It's a saddle, okay?" I cleared my throat. "For educational purposes. I was teaching them about the customs of the Earth rodeo."

"Seriously?" Amy's eyes narrowed as she noticed Snarffle's footprints on the wall and the lamp he had knocked over. "David, you were supposed to entertain them, not try to kill them."

I shrugged. "With boys, it's pretty much the same thing." Amy didn't really think that was funny. I pressed on. "Come on, look at all the pillows. It's fine."

She sighed. "Look, I know you don't want to hear this—and I know my dad takes it way too far—but without your grandma here, I think we need to be extra responsible."

"You don't think I'm responsible?" *Remember when I saved the world that one time? Like, last week?*

Amy gestured at the messy room. "You tell me." Then she crossed her arms over her chest in a gesture that reminded me of a certain Head of Security around here. Whose side was she on, anyway?

"Just because you were working here all school year while I was back in Florida doesn't mean you're any better than—"

"Oh, please, David. I'm not saying anything like that. I just...when I asked you to think of something gender-appropriate, I didn't mean that you should—"

"But this is what gender-appropriate means! It's the kind of thing boys like. On any planet."

Amy rolled her eyes. "Fine. But that doesn't make it—"

"Hey, that looks kind of like a saddle for a flubble beast." One of the girl aliens—a squat little thing with shiny pink skin—poked her head around Amy's leg. "Are they *riding* Snarffle? Really?"

The three girls squealed and rushed past Amy, spilling into the rec room.

"Can I go next?"

"No, me!"

"I bet we'll be better at riding him than any of the boys."

"Yeah!"

Even timid little Kandeel seemed excited by the prospect. I think Snarffle was the only thing she liked about this planet.

I smirked at Amy. It was difficult to keep myself from saying *I told you so*, but I managed. "What can I say? I guess awesomeness knows no gender."

To her credit, Amy smiled back. "It actually does look pretty fun."

I really shouldn't blame her for being related to Tate—it's not like she had a choice in the matter.

"Sorry I got mad," I said.

"Me too."

Kanduu stepped between us. "Are you going to do that

thing now where human males and females mash their faces together, connected by their speech organs?"

"Yeah! We saw you two doing that behind a tree in the backyard yesterday," one of the slime-drippers said. "It was hilarious!"

All the kids buzzed with laughter and made exaggerated kissy-faces. Amy's face turned as red as mine felt.

"Let's just play the game, okay?" I said, probably too loud. "Who's next?"

So it became the Boys vs. Girls Rodeo Roundup. All the kids took turns, and we put up a sheet of paper to post the times, and there was lots of cheering and booing and general craziness. It was the best time anyone had had since Grandma left.

Until Tate burst into the room, his face white and his breathing ragged.

Great. I braced myself for a lecture, wondering how many of the new rules we had managed to violate in one afternoon.

But Tate hardly seemed to notice the mess, or the saddle, or anything else in the room.

"Dad?" Amy's voice was concerned. "What's wrong?"

But he looked right at me instead. "It's your grandmother. She's in danger."

9

Amy and I rushed after Tate down the hallway, spouting questions that he waved away.

"You gotta see it for yourself."

"See what?" we asked.

"You'll see."

We followed him into the sitting room. He pointed at Grandma's ancient TV, encased in a wooden frame just like the stereo was. It's hardly ever on, so I had sort of forgotten it was even there.

Tate crossed his arms over his chest and stared at the blank screen. Ever since Grandma had left, his nasty habit of chewing on toothpicks had gotten worse, and a soggy one hung out the side of his mouth. He was chomping them so hard he was probably going through two boxes a day.

The screen remained black. "Dad?" Amy said after a few quiet moments. "Is there a reason we're—"

"Hush." He pointed at the TV again, as if we were having trouble locating it.

So we looked at the blank screen with him. An awkward minute passed. Then another. I cleared my throat. "Um... you know that you need to actually turn it on if you want to watch some—"

"Hush!"

A few moments later the screen glowed without anyone hitting the power switch. Weird. The image was fuzzy and the sound was just a static hiss. I was starting to get some serious horror movie vibes.

"Watch this," Tate said. *As if we had a choice.* "It comes on every couple a minutes."

A shape drifted into half focus. I figured we must have been looking at an alien, because its clothing was all loops and swirls and pinwheels, a crazy-looking getup that no human would ever consider putting on—

"It's your grandma!" said Amy.

—except maybe *that* human.

I squinted. Amy was right. The picture sharpened a bit, and there was Grandma, smiling and waving right at us in that weird outfit. It looked like she was really getting into the spirit of her extraterrestrial holiday.

Then her lips started moving, but no sound came out. The image skipped, jagged lines of interference jumping all around the screen. When Tate banged the side of the TV with his fist, the audio crackled and we could make out snippets of Grandma's message.

"... don't know if you're receiving this, but wanted to tell you ... they're keeping me ... shortage of food ... miss you all ... can't wait ... forget about me!"

She smiled and waved some more, all her flamboyant accessories bouncing and rattling around her head and shoulders, and then the picture cut out entirely.

"You had me worried there for a minute, Dad." Amy let out a sigh of relief. "It's really good to see her, but I wish the sound wasn't so spotty. Oh, I can't wait to hear all about the trip when she gets back!"

"I wonder how they're transmitting the message." I tilted my head and studied the TV. "That's so cool."

Tate stared at us as if we had just suggested he set fire to the house.

"Don't you get it?" he said. "That was a distress call. Plain and simple."

"You think?" I said. "She looked pretty happy to me."

"Come on, Dad. Not everything is a crime scene."

Tate pulled a mini spiral notebook out of his pocket, a holdover from his law enforcement days, and then he waved at the TV. "This keeps repeating. I watched it three times before I got you two. Took notes." He ran a finger over the paper. "She says *they're keeping me*, then it cuts out, and then she says something about a *shortage of food.*"

He paused dramatically and stared at us, eyebrows raised, apparently inviting us to connect the invisible dots.

"So?" I finally said. "That could mean anything. Or nothing."

"Probably nothing, Dad."

"Oh, come on!" He threw his hands in the air. "Didn't you ever watch those old *Twilight Zone* shows? The classic episode where the UFO comes, and everyone thinks the aliens are all nice and friendly just because they have a book called *To Serve Man*, so a bunch of humans get on the UFO to go see the aliens' home planet, only the main guy figures out that *To Serve Man* is really a cookbook, and that means—"

Amy and I burst out laughing.

"Dad. Do you really think they want to *eat* her? Seriously?"

"It's not funny, young lady. I wouldn't put anything past that shiny Sillyfalls fella; didn't trust him one bit. Why, this whole awards scam could be a way to lure folks off their planets for a big feast. *Shortage of food*, indeed." Tate consulted his notes again. "And he kept saying they wanted to see her in the flesh. You notice that?" He jabbed at his notebook. "Said it two or three different times. *In the flesh*. Like she was some kind of delicacy."

"Dad, it's a figure of speech, that's all, and besides—"

"And they didn't give her any time to pack. That's mighty fishy to me, sending someone away for a week with no time to pack any clothes." His frown deepened. "Of course, you don't worry about what somebody's wearing when you're fixing to eat them."

"But Dad, it looks like they found her an outfit that would be suitable for—"

"Then she spells it out for us." He jabbed his finger at the TV again for emphasis. "*Can't wait*, she says. Like we can't wait to do something for her. We've got to do it now."

"Mr. Tate, that might not be—"

"But it's the last part that kills me. *Forget about me*, she says. She wants us to forge ahead with the business, be good caretakers of her life's work. *Forget about me*," he repeated, shaking his head slowly and looking at the floor. "We've had our differences, to be sure, but I have to say that is one brave lady."

What was wrong with him? "You have to admit, Mr. Tate, she didn't look like she was in danger. You know . . . the smiling? The waving?"

Tate harrumphed. "Haven't you ever seen those phony messages from prisoners of war on the news? Never trust a video. If you were being held hostage and some space creature had a laser gun pointed at you off-camera, I reckon you'd do or say whatever it wanted."

"But Dad, she's not a hostage," Amy said. "Think about it: Mr. Harnox was there. He's, like, the nicest guy in the universe. It couldn't have been a trap."

Tate sniffed and shook his head. "Those were holograms or something. Can't be trusted. No fancy-pants alien is going to snow me with a lot of shiny technology like I was some kind of country rube."

"Okay, whatever." I shrugged. "I guess we'll just have to wait until Grandma gets back and she can settle this."

"Negative. The situation is dire. *Can't wait*, remember? She may need help immediately."

"What do you plan on doing from here, exactly?"

"Nothing can be done from here." Tate hiked up his belt and squared his shoulders. "That's why I'm going to get her. Right now."

10

Amy and I stared at each other while Tate stomped off toward the staircase.

"Did he just say—?"

"Do you think he'll really...?"

Tate's boots hit the first step with a *boom*. He called to us over his shoulder as he pounded up the stairs. "Follow me. We've got a couple things to talk about before I leave." Soon he was on the second floor, out of sight.

We had no choice but to obey. When we were halfway up I noticed the group of alien kids, with Snarffle packed in the middle of their colorful circle, peeking at us from around the corner of the hallway.

"Is the puffy, red-faced human angry again?" Kanduu whispered.

"It's okay," I said. "Just wait for us in the rec room."

"But no rodeo until we get back," Amy said in passing. The kids groaned.

Tate was rummaging through a chest of drawers in the guest room he used as an office/bedroom. We stopped in the doorway.

"Mr. Tate—sir—maybe you should, you know, slow down. Think about this for a minute," I coaxed. Something told me he wasn't going to be as good as Grandma at fitting in off-world. "You're probably jumping to conclusions. I mean, it doesn't seem like she's in any real danger." *And she's certainly not going to be too happy to see* you *in the middle of her big alien celebration.*

But wait—was I actually trying to talk Tate out of leaving? Wouldn't it be a lot better with him gone?

It was pretty easy to decide to stop trying to persuade him.

"Dad, maybe we should wait and see if her message comes through any clearer. Or if she tries to send another one."

Tate ignored her as he continued to rifle through the drawers.

I know Amy was just as confident as I was when it came to running this place, but she must have been worried about her dad. She took a few small steps into the room. "Please stop and think. This whole thing could just be a big misunder—"

"Here it is!" Tate held up a shiny badge. "Let's see if they want to mess with an official employee of the Intergalactic Police Force!" An alien law enforcement authority named Commander Rezzlurr had given that to Tate last summer when he was hired to be Grandma's Head of Security. Tate proudly pinned it to his chest.

Then he took his old wide-brimmed sheriff's hat down from a peg on the wall and placed it on his head just so, checking his reflection in the mirror.

"But how do you even plan on finding her?" Amy said.

"Oh, I'm prepared on that account." Tate gestured to the transporter in the corner. "I've interrogated more than a few alien Tourists about these things. A good lawman learns everything he can about his environment." He took out his little notebook again. "Let's see . . . so when you step through here, apparently you end up at some central processing station, and from there you can catch another transporter to anywhere. And I wrote down the name of the planet that Slippyfangs was talking about, you bet I did."

Tate looked at the transporter, took a deep breath, then turned his attention to us. "Now listen good. I won't be gone long. Just gonna grab her and come back, no foolin' around." He rapped the transporter door with a knuckle. "From what I gather, these things work lickety-split. I don't expect to be gone more'n an hour or two." Tate patted his wide belly. "Why, it wouldn't surprise me if your grandma cooks us up a nice big meal tonight, right here where she belongs."

"An hour or two?" Amy said. "I don't know, Dad, that might be too optimistic."

"Yeah, Mr. Tate. I'm guessing interplanetary travel is a little more complex than that, even by transporter."

Tate raised his eyebrows. "Only took your grandma a few seconds to get there while you all just milled around in the kitchen and let it happen."

"But those were aliens who knew what they were doing —they've probably used the transporters a hundred times," I said.

"For all we know they rigged the system to take her directly there," Amy added. "It could be set up totally different now."

But he just waved us off. Tate had obviously made up his mind in that way adults do when they stop listening to reason.

"I'll be back with your grandma before she even has time to thank me."

I doubted *thank* would be the right word. "Mr. Tate, you better hope she really is in danger. Because if she's not, and you go barging in there..."

Tate's eyes narrowed. "You let me worry about that, boy." He took the toothpick out of his mouth and pointed it at us. "Now, here's the one rule that matters: None of these aliens puts so much as one scaly foot outside the b-and-b until we return, you follow me?"

"There's hardly anyone left around here, anyway," I muttered under my breath.

I thought maybe Tate heard that, because he glared at me, but then he looked back and forth between Amy and me a few times. "And you"—he leaned down until we were face-to-face—"don't go getting any ideas."

"About what?"

He straightened back up and looked at Amy again. "About anything."

Yikes. Awkward. I pretended to study something on the floor until Tate turned and faced the transporter.

Amy sighed. "If you're really going to go through with this . . . then good luck, Dad."

"A good lawman doesn't rely on luck," he said. Then he took off his hat, bent down, and kissed her on the forehead. "But I appreciate the sentiment, little lady."

He faced the door, took a deep breath, and grabbed the handle. He grunted. It wouldn't budge.

"Dad, you need to—"

"Give me some room." Tate pulled again, first with one hand and then two. He stopped, wiped his palms on his pants, then lifted his leg and put one of his big boots on the wall next to the door for leverage. He leaned backward and yanked on the handle, putting his whole body into it. His face contorted into a grimace, and his shoulders shook while sweat dripped down his temple. There was much gasping and wheezing. He finally let go, taking off his hat to wipe the beads of moisture off his forehead.

Amy stepped forward. "You have to turn this little latch. Right here." She did, and the door swung open easily.

"I knew that," Tate said. Then he stepped inside the transporter, the circle on the front of the door flashed blue, and he was gone.

We just stood there for a few moments. It seemed extra quiet without Tate blundering around.

Amy sighed. "Isn't he sweet?"

"Who?"

She elbowed me in the ribs. "My dad, obviously."

"Ummm...*sweet* isn't really the first word that comes to mind." *It's not really in the top one hundred, either.*

"He's actually going to a different planet, filled with all of those"—she did a gruff impersonation of her dad—"*alien germs and microbes and who-knows-what* he's always complaining about. Think about it: even though stepping through that transporter has to be the thing that freaks him out the most, he's going through with it because he's worried about her. I think he really cares for her. That's as romantic as my dad ever gets."

O—kay...that was not somewhere my mind was going to let itself go. Time to just change the subject.

"So...what are we going to do now?" I was suddenly very aware that her dad was no longer lurking around, watching us like a big, sweaty hawk.

Amy looked at me and smiled, a really big one that crinkled up the cute little freckles on her nose. Wait—was she thinking what I was thinking?

"We're all alone," she said.

She *was* thinking what I was thinking!

"Do you know what this means?" she said.

Yes, I did! "I think so..." I said, moving a little closer.

"It means that we are officially in charge of the bed-and-breakfast."

Oh. So I guess she was *not* thinking what I was thinking.

"It's like a dream come true!" She twirled around, sweeping

her hands through the air to indicate the entire house. It was —eerily—a very Grandma-like gesture.

And suddenly not even I was thinking what I was thinking anymore.

"Let's go check on the kids," Amy said. "Then I'll get started on dinner. You can visit the adult Tourists and tell them what's going on." She beamed, her smile almost too big for her face. "We're really in charge!"

She was right.

It was just us, all alone, completely in charge of the biggest secret on the entire planet.

This was going to be awesome.

When we walked down the stairs, the first thing we saw was the group of alien kids huddled around the TV. Kanduu was standing on Lizard Boy's shoulders, fiddling with something on top of the screen.

"What are you guys doing?" I said.

"Fixing your primitive little communication toy," one of the slime-drippers said.

"It wasn't equipped to deal with the volume of information streaming in, so we made a few modifications," the other one said.

It's always nice to feel like a moron because you can't follow what a second grader is saying.

Kanduu hopped down, and we could see their handiwork. Sticking up from the top of the TV was a multipronged antenna made from a pile of silverware and metallic kitchen appliances, all held together by duct tape and aluminum foil.

"It should work better now," little Kandeel squeaked.

They backed away from the screen, and there was Grandma in that bizarre getup, smiling and waving, only this time the image was crystal clear.

"Hello, everyone! I don't know if you're receiving this, but I wanted to tell you that I'm having a fabulous time! They're keeping me entertained, and there's certainly no shortage of food, friends, or fun! I miss everyone terribly—yes, even you, Tate—and I can't wait to see you all again! I know I'm truly blessed, because I can relax and enjoy it all, knowing the b-and-b is in good hands. But I'll be back soon, so don't you dare forget about me!"

Amy clapped her hands and gave me a quick hug. "Oh, I'm so glad to know she's all right."

"Of course she is." I couldn't help but laugh. "And I hope your dad is enjoying his little excursion."

11

The rest of that afternoon was about as fun as it could be, given that we were still trapped inside by Tate's lame orders. Amy made sandwiches and lemonade for everyone, and then the alien kids taught us a game called Lammaarang, which involved lots of random hopping and a big puddle of mayonnaise for some reason.

I think Mrs. Crowzen was glad for the break. She slopped mud all over her shells and lounged under some giant ferns in the woods out back. She told me she was doing it to cool off, but I think she just wanted to hide from the kids. And the rest of the adult Tourists seemed to be in a better mood (probably because no oversize earthling was shouting at them).

It was nothing special, I guess, but it seemed more fun because Amy and I were in charge. After everything we'd been through together, we were good at taking care of the Tourists by now. We could run this whole operation by ourselves, and that was a pretty cool feeling.

But then it started to get dark. And Tate hadn't returned yet.

Now, I haven't been afraid of the dark since I was a little kid. But, as I watched the world fade to black outside the windows, something about knowing we were responsible for protecting intergalactic visitors from whatever might be out there, was—okay, I admit—a little freaky.

And I was wondering if Amy was starting to worry about her dad, who had definitely not returned after an hour or two. She kept it together while we helped the kids get ready for bed, and later, when we delivered tea to the adult Tourists in their rooms. But after the house was all settled down, I found her in the second floor lounge, crouched down in front of a window with just her eyes peeking above the sill.

"What are you doing?"

"Come over here." She kept her voice very low and didn't turn around to look at me. "But stay down."

I crawled over to the window and knelt beside her.

"Do you see that station wagon parked down there? Just before the street curves toward town?"

I could make out the windshield, but the rest was hidden behind the trees in the bend of the road.

"Yes," I said. "But why are we whispering? Can the car hear us?"

She smacked me in the arm by way of an answer. "Don't you think it's weird for a car to just be sitting there? It's not like it belongs to one of our customers."

I thought for a few moments. "Maybe whoever was driving it is at the park? It's a short walk from here."

"At night? I don't think so."

"Good point."

"Plus, it's been there since I woke up this morning."

"Oh."

"And I swear I saw it yesterday too. Same place."

"Oh."

Another smack in the arm. "Good observations, David. Very helpful."

"What am I supposed to do?"

"Okay, don't laugh. But I can't help shake the feeling..." She trailed off and chewed on her lower lip.

"What?"

She shook her head. "Never mind. You'll just laugh. You won't believe me."

"Amy, we just put a dozen space aliens to bed with tea and footie pajamas. I'd believe almost anything."

"Okay...for the last couple of days...I can't help feeling that we're being watched, somehow. I can't prove it or anything, but I—"

"Oh, I'm so glad it's not just me."

"Really?" She clutched my arm. "You feel it too?"

I told her about the hot air balloon that had been hovering around, with maybe somebody up there taking pictures.

Her eyes got wide. "That is not good. Do you think it's the same people we met on the Fourth of July?"

"I don't know. Maybe." I snuck another peek at the car. "I'm not always the biggest fan of your dad's tactics, but I'm pretty glad he put up all of those fake security cameras outside. Maybe it'll keep them away."

Amy sighed. "I wish Barzo was here."

"Who's Bozo?"

"*Barzo.* You know, that guy our age who comes to the b-and-b with his parents sometimes?"

Great. So he had a name. Earlier this summer, Amy had told me that she'd made friends with an alien. She went on and on about how cool he was.

I know it might sound weird, but I was kind of worried that she might like him. You know, as in, *like* him.

"David . . . is anything the matter?"

"What? With me? No. Why would there be?" I shook my head a little harder than was probably necessary. "It's just . . . I mean, why would you want him to be here? Does he have the magical alien ability to see through station wagon doors so we could find out who's inside?"

"Kind of."

What? "Really?"

"Well, I think I told you about all of these cool gadgets that he brings with him. He had a couple of little earpieces, and you could hear what anyone was saying, no matter how far away they were." She looked off into the distance and smiled at some memory. "One time we were hanging out at the park, and there was this group of kids way at the other end. It was so funny when he—"

"Got it. Oh, well. Too bad he's not here."

She gave me a funny look. "What is your deal? What's wrong tonight?"

I waved at the window. "Bozo's not here, so there's no point in talking about it. He can't help us."

"Fine. So what do you suggest we do?"

I peeked out the window again. "Maybe it's nothing. I'm trying not to be paranoid just because we're here alone, you know? I mean, the evidence is not the greatest. What do we really have here, anyway? A rubber ear, a hot air balloon, and a car that's parked on a public street. There could be lots of explanations for—"

I was interrupted by a noise. Downstairs.

We froze. There wasn't supposed to be anybody downstairs.

"Did you—?"

"Shhhh."

There it was again. A voice. Definitely a male. And then more voices, fainter, but distinct.

No aliens had passed us to go downstairs. The only explanation could be humans. Someone had gotten into the B&B. Multiple someones. Had they really been keeping the house under surveillance? Were they finally going to make their move?

I never dreamed I could miss Tate so badly.

"We have to go check it out," Amy whispered.

"I know."

Neither one of us moved.

"Seriously, it's just us now. We have to go down there."

I took a deep breath. "Okay. I'll go first."

"Why you?"

"Because I'm the boy."

"So? I beat you at arm wrestling, like, three times in a row yesterday."

"You seriously think whoever is down there wants to arm wrestle?"

"No, I just—"

"Fine. You go first."

More noise from downstairs. We froze again, ears cocked toward the staircase. Wait...was that music? I didn't think the characters in horror movies were supposed to be able to hear the creepy sound track. This was getting worse.

Amy made a shooing motion at me. "Okay. You can go first."

"Thanks a lot." I slowly got to my feet and tiptoed toward the stairs, Amy right behind me. I skipped the squeaky third step, holding my breath.

The voice yelled something, sounding angry. I grabbed the banister with both hands, trying to figure out what to do.

"Wait—that sounds like my dad!" Amy pushed past me and ran down to the sitting room.

The TV was back on, casting a blue glow over the dark room. Sure enough, Tate's jowly face nearly filled up the whole screen.

"...hope you kids are getting this message. I don't trust these fancy contraptions one bit. And it makes me furious to report that I am trapped—"

"Did he say trapped?" Amy dug her fingernails into my arm. "Oh, no."

"—on some kind of a, well… I guess on Earth you'd call it a dang luxury cruise ship."

I burst out laughing. Amy relaxed her death grip on my forearm.

A gaggle of brightly dressed aliens flitted across the screen behind Tate. They were talking and laughing and gesturing all over with their antennae and tentacles. Tate turned his head and shouted at them, "Would you all quiet down! I'm trying to make a durn phone call."

A willowy alien turned to face him. "What's a phone?"

"Whatever you call this setup here." Tate waved a hand at the screen, frowning under his bushy mustache. "This… this… oh, never mind. Just give me a little quiet."

That group of aliens moved on, but were quickly replaced by another colorful cluster. They were was apparently on their way to some kind of dance, because music started blaring, and the aliens looked like they were moving in a levitating conga line. Tate had stumbled on to quite the space bash.

He hunched over, blocking our view of the aliens with his burly shoulders, and yelled over the music, "I gave the person in charge the name of the planet I was aiming for, and they sent me to some lineup. Thought I was waiting for a transporter, and turned out I was getting on this crazy cruise ship."

He glanced over his shoulder at the partying aliens, shook his head in disgust, and turned back to the screen. "So we're headed to that planet your grandma's on, but we're going what they call 'the old-fashioned way,' sailing among the stars instead of using transporters. Sounds like it's going to take several days to get there."

Amy and I looked at each other, eyebrows raised.

"That means you two are in charge until I can get back. I'm right sorry about putting you in this position, but I know you'll make me proud." He leaned forward even more, his face in extreme close-up. "Won't you?"

I nodded automatically, but of course he couldn't see us.

"You need to shut down the transporters so you don't get a bunch of guests coming in, then hunker down and wait until I get back in touch and tell you when I can make it home, understand?" He paused to let that sink in before continuing. "You take care of yourself, little lady." Then his expression soured, and the glare he directed at the screen was unmistakably meant for me. "And you take care of her too, boy." The music blasted even louder, and glittery confetti swirled all around Tate's head. His shoulders slumped a little, and we could see the cosmic conga line hovering and weaving around just behind him.

Tate shook his head. Now there were sparkly pieces of confetti all over his sheriff's hat and stuck in his mustache. He started to say something, but it was much lower, as though he was talking to himself. The dancers thinned out and the music became muted, and we could hear what he was muttering.

"... couldn't have ended up with a group of aliens working on some big, important project, could I? Or on Commander Rezzlurr's police-precinct ship, where I could actually learn a useful thing or two. Oh no, of course not." Tate glanced back at the last few extraterrestrial dancers. He sighed heavily, his shoulders slumped even more. "Nope. Wherever I go, it's always aliens on vacation."

The picture cut out for a moment, and when it started over at the beginning of the message, I turned the sound down. Amy looked over at me. "Don't say it."

"Say what?"

"Anything."

But soon a grin crept across her face. "Oh, I guess it is pretty funny, isn't it? My dad stuck somewhere like that?"

I nodded. "I can't even picture him on a cruise ship on Earth, much less one where he's surrounded by aliens that he can't get away from."

Amy was quiet for a moment, looking around the room. "So I guess it is official. We're actually running this place for longer than just a day." She shook her head in wonder. "Who knows? It might be as long as a week."

"Yep." I looked over at her. "I can't think of anyone I'd rather do that job with."

"Thanks. Me neither."

Amy smiled. I guess every once in a great while I get lucky and sort of say the right thing.

But then she yawned. "We should probably get some sleep. We're going to need our energy for tomorrow."

"I know." I walked over to the window and pushed aside the curtain a little bit. "But first let's see what's going on out there."

"Good idea."

Amy came to stand beside me, and we looked out the window together. But the street was empty.

The mystery car was gone.

12

During breakfast the next morning, Amy and I filled the Tourists in on the latest developments. In the least surprising news ever, no one was heartbroken over Tate's prolonged absence.

While we were washing the dishes, Mrs. Crowzen came to see us, her crablike claws clicking on the kitchen tiles.

"Excuse me for interrupting, but I have a request," she said, not quite looking at us. "On behalf of the children, of course."

"Sure. What can we do for you?" Amy said, drying her hands on a dish towel.

"Well, you see . . . I'm a bit worried about reporting back to my school's administrators—to say nothing of the children's parents, but don't get me started on *them*—as my objectives for this off-world excursion were very clear. The students have a list of things to experience: observe the natives interacting in a social setting, visit a place where Earth commerce is being conducted, that type of thing."

Amy and I glanced at each other. "You want to take the kids into town," I said.

"Indeed." Mrs. Crowzen rummaged around in a purse she had gotten from one of Grandma's trunks of used clothing. "When I made the reservations," she said, holding up a paper she had taken from the purse, "I was assured that there would be very few restrictions on that type of activity—as long as we took the proper precautions, of course."

"I know. We're really sorry," Amy said. "It's normally no problem at all, but this has been a very unusual week for us."

"I see." Mrs. Crowzen studied the floor. She started to leave, got almost through the doorway, then turned back to us and took a deep breath. "Now, I would hate to file a complaint with the Interstellar Tourism Bureau, especially with that adorable earthling receiving her big award right now, but, well, I'm afraid that if I do not complete my objectives . . ." She clacked her claws together nervously. "That is to say, if I cannot . . ."

Suddenly she let out a wail and shuddered all over. She plopped down heavily in one of the wooden kitchen chairs and moisture leaked out from everywhere—eyes, ears, mouth, the little cracks between the exoskeleton plates of her body, everywhere. I'm no astrobiologist, but I'm pretty sure that must be how people cry on her planet.

I never know what to do when somebody is crying. Thankfully, Amy was there. She brought Mrs. Crowzen a couple of dish towels (this was definitely a bigger job than Kleenex could handle) and patted her on the back.

"Oh, I'm so sorry," Amy said soothingly.

Mrs. Crowzen heaved a couple more sobs before settling down. "Please forgive me. It's just that, well, these parents pay a lot of money for their children's education, you see. And sometimes they can get a little bit ill-tempered...perhaps more than a little bit...and I just cannot..."

She clunked her head down on the table and left it there. More wailing. More sobbing. Lots more leaking.

I caught Amy's eye and inclined my head toward the door. She nodded, then handed Mrs. Crowzen a couple more towels. "Please excuse us for a moment."

We met in the hallway. "We need to let her take them out," I said.

"You know we can't do that."

"Amy, she's going to get fired or something if we don't. And this is obviously not the best time for anyone to be filing a complaint with the Tourism Bureau. What if they send some kind of inspector to check it out? We're probably in violation of at least a dozen intergalactic child-labor laws."

"What about..." Amy gestured toward the window facing the street. "You know, what we talked about last night?"

"I checked first thing this morning. That car is still gone. And no hot air balloons anywhere." I watched her as she thought it over. "There's a chance we might have been overly suspicious. After what we went through with Scratchull I guess it's understandable, but not everyone is trying to blow up the planet, you know? We can't be afraid of everything."

Amy glanced at the kitchen door and then back at me, her face twisted with indecision. "Do you know how mad my dad would be if he found out we let them go?"

"Do you know how mad my grandma would be if she found out your dad had invented all these harsh rules in the first place?"

Amy bit her lower lip. "Okay, you have a point . . . but I just don't know if we should risk it."

Fresh wails drifted out the kitchen door. This is not how I wanted to spend the rest of the week. "Look, you see your job here as a—whaddayacallit—an apprenticeship. Right?"

"What do you mean?"

"Grandma's going to retire someday, or decide that she'd like to take another spin in the transporter and not come back, or whatever. The point is, she's going to be done with this place eventually. Right?"

Amy nodded, eyeing me carefully.

"Well, it's not like she can turn the business over to just anyone. Don't you want it to be you? I mean, isn't that kind of your dream, to run this place someday?"

Amy sighed. "Is it that obvious?"

"Only for people with eyes."

She blushed. "I'm sorry, David. I should have talked to you first, of course. After all, she is your grandma. So this should be, like, your inheritance, right? I mean, if I—"

I held up my hand to stop her. We did not need to have this conversation right now. "Look, don't worry about it. I just meant you should get some realistic practice at running the place."

"But isn't it your dream, too? I mean, this place is so amazing, don't you want to live here the rest of your life and soak up every moment?"

Just then the slime-drippers ran by, screaming and laughing, spraying snotty goo droplets everywhere with their flailing limbs. Snarffle rounded the corner, a crazed smile stretching his face, clearly relishing the chase. He caught up with them at the end of the hall, his beach-ball body knocking them down like bowling pins. The kids grabbed on and rolled with Snarffle, smashing into an end table and shattering the vase on top. The action stopped when they slammed into the wall and sprawled out on the floor, panting and grinning in a slime-covered mess that would have to be cleaned up. Probably by me.

I looked back at Amy. "Not really."

"Are you serious?"

"Look, Forest Grove is a great place to visit—"

"—you just wouldn't want to live here?" She seemed pretty disappointed.

"Honestly? I don't know yet. I mean, I'm in middle school."

"But this is different—do you know how many people all over the planet would want to know about a place like this? Millions!"

"Don't get me wrong. I love it here. But you've always known what you want to do with your life. Even before you knew about this place, you told me you wanted to be an astrobiologist and study about outer space and all of that when you went to college, remember?"

She nodded.

"I think that's really cool for you, but I just...I don't know. I need more time to figure out what I'm going to do with the rest of my life."

"Okay." She smiled. "But whatever happens, you have to promise that you'll visit a lot."

The kids picked themselves up and ran to the stairs, spraying slime everywhere once again, with Snarffle in hot pursuit.

"Who could resist?"

Amy grinned and shook her head as she watched them head up to the second floor. Then she took a deep breath and looked back at me. "Okay. You're right. Your grandma would want us to provide the best Earth experience possible for her guests."

"Now you're talking."

"Who are we to stand in the way of her life's work?"

"Exactly."

"But someone should stay here to watch the house, and the other one should definitely chaperone." The hopeful look in her eyes was unmistakable, even for me, who's no good at reading girls.

"I'll stay here," I said.

"Are you sure? Because I don't mind if—"

"Come on. I think you probably know Forest Grove a little bit better than I do. You'll be more of a tour guide than just a chaperone."

"Thanks, David!" She gave me a big hug and then bounced up and down like Snarffle at walk time as we made our way back to the kitchen.

"Mrs. Crowzen? We've decided that you can take the kids into town for their field trip."

"Oh, that's wonderful!" Her face brightened and all that tear moisture got sucked back into her shell like she had a vacuum under there. Cool trick.

"You just need to let us help with the disguises."

· ☙ ·

Half an hour later, all eight kids were lined up in the sitting room, waiting to head out. I have to admit, we did a pretty decent job on their earthling disguises.

Grandma didn't have any dresses big enough to fit over Mrs. Crowzen's roundish crab-shell body. So we took a king-size bedsheet with a floral pattern and cut out head- and armholes. A floppy sun hat, a long pair of lady gloves that went past the elbow, and a ton of makeup took care of the rest. She looked like a fat lady with a clown face in a muumuu, but at least she looked human.

For the girls with antennae growing out of the tops of their heads, Amy pulled the growths together and bound them with scrunchies. "There you go. Just looks like you're wearing pigtails now."

"Pigtails?" said Kanduu, who was watching.

"Yeah, they're really cute. Lots of girls on Earth wear them."

"But *pig*tails? Seriously?" Kanduu tilted his head and studied his girl classmates. "So you're saying their heads look like the butt of a dirty farm animal?"

"What? No, that's just a figure of—"

"Earthlings are weird. That's worse than corn *dog*." He jotted down a quick entry in his notebook.

"Just leave it alone," I whispered to Amy.

Long sleeves, ankle-length dresses or baggy sweats, and oversize hats took care of most of the class. The slime-drippers, however, presented more of a challenge. We put them in XL nylon sweat suits; when the slime leaked through we tried covering their bodies in Saran Wrap under their clothes. Not good. Finally, even Mrs. Crowzen admitted that it just wasn't going to work.

"I'm afraid you boys will have to stay here during the field trip," she told them.

"No way!"

"We've been stuck inside for days!"

"It's just too risky." Mrs. Crowzen shook her head. "You'd be putting the rest of the group in danger, and compromising the security of our hosts."

"But can't we—"

"No."

The slime-drippers looked at each other. Then they whispered in each other's ears. Finally, they both nodded at the same time. They wiped the slime from their bodies and shook it off their hands in yellowish-green gobs that spattered the floor.

"How's this?"

They were both totally dry, and without the slime oozing out from everywhere, they looked really humanoid. Hardly needed a disguise at all—just a hat to cover the antennae.

"What happened?" I said.

One of them grinned sheepishly. "We can sort of control it. Sometimes."

The other laughed out loud. "We can totally control it. Always."

Amy looked confused. "Then why would you *choose* to walk around covered in slime?"

"Because it's awesome!"

"Yeah, we love this planet."

"How mortifying." Mrs. Crowzen huffed and clacked her claws. "First, you will apologize to our guests for the deception, and then you will stay here as a punishment and—"

"It's okay," I said. "They'll fit right in. I don't know a single Earth boy their age who would have done anything any different." I didn't add *including me*, though, because Amy looked as appalled as Mrs. Crowzen. "You all go out and have fun. Just be back before six o'clock, okay? We'll have dinner ready then."

The other kids had drifted away and were messing around in the sitting room. Mrs. Crowzen made that horrible screeching sound by rubbing her claw on her chest plate, and the little aliens rushed over and lined up single file in the entryway.

Amy took her place up front as the leader of the excursion. She pulled out a sheaf of notes and cleared her throat as they marched out the front door. "Forest Grove was founded one Earth-century ago, with the primary industry being fur trapping and logging, sending goods by river to the larger city of Bellingham." She led them down the steps. "The third mayor of the new town was Martha VanDeBosch, making this the first town in the Pacific Northwest to elect a woman to that position." She paused halfway down the front path and looked at the kids. "You're probably going to want to write this stuff down." The kids stifled groans as they hauled out their notebooks. Then they were off, Amy lecturing away. I smiled and shut the door.

The next couple of hours were pretty uneventful. The Arkamendian Air Painters asked to go out. There was really no way to disguise them, but they just wanted to hike up to one of their secluded meadows. I could hardly say no after letting the kids out, so off they went. Then Cottage Cheese Head and the Blob pressed their case to be allowed to go fishing down at the river.

"I don't know, guys. I mean, I guess we could throw a big fishing hat and some sunglasses on you." I pointed to Cottage Cheese Man. "But you…" I sized up the Blob. "I just don't think we can make you look humanoid enough. Do you, uh, mind telling me why you even picked this spot for vacation? I mean, you knew it was a primitive planet that required a disguise, right?"

The Blob chuckled. "Let's show him." Cottage Cheese Head grabbed one of the Blob's stumpy arms and pulled. The thing stretched like taffy until it was the approximate length and width of a human arm. After doing the same with the other one, he went to work on the torso, kneading and pulling the blobby mass into a more elongated, thinner shape. It looked like he was molding a huge pile of sculptor's clay.

"Little help with the legs?" the Blob said. I knelt down and grabbed a handful of his squishy flesh (I had kind of gotten used to that disgusting feeling last summer). He had a wide base of solidified jelly that he slithered around on, so I had to tug hard to create the legs from scratch. And making the knees was difficult; they came out pretty knobby. But in the end I think I did a pretty good job.

The Blob stood up. He was a little shaky on his new limbs, but a lot taller and more humanoid. Man, I wish I could do that to my body before basketball season started. I'd transform from point guard to power forward in five minutes.

"Will you stay like that?"

"For a few hours, anyway. After that, everything will sort of melt back into position." He marched in little circles, getting used to his new body. He kind of jiggled when he moved, but then again so did a lot of earthlings. I thought he could pass.

"All right, fellas. Grab some clothes and you're good to go."

They were the last of the Tourists, so now the house was empty. I cleaned up the breakfast stuff and made a few beds in the guest rooms. Then I fed Snarffle, and he curled up on the bed in my room for one of his naps.

So I was all alone in that big house when someone started pounding on the front door like they were trying to knock it off its hinges.

13

I looked out the peephole.

Aliens.

The tall one had dusky yellow skin with an enormous round nose and spiky hair. The short one had the same nose, but more of an orange tint. She either had an antigravity beehive hairdo or else there was a traffic cone on her head. And they both had decided to go with the silvery one-piece-jumpsuit look.

The male continued to beat on the door while the little female peeked in the windows. Both of them cast nervous glances back down the road toward town, but the street was empty, as usual.

Leaning my shoulder against the door, I scanned a mental list of the Tourists I'd met so far this summer. It's hard to keep track of all the aliens that come through here, but I was pretty sure I'd never seen these two. Although I might have met someone from their planet; there was something vaguely familiar about them.

More pounding. What was going on? Maybe they had checked in with someone else a few days ago and then had gone out and gotten lost? That didn't seem right. Tate would have kept records of—

"Please! Help us!"

I looked through the peephole again. The female was calling through cupped hands pressed against the window.

I cracked the door open a few inches, careful to block the jamb with my shoe so they couldn't burst in.

"Oh, thank the stars," the female said. "Quick, open up and let us in."

Not yet. "What's going on?"

The male wedged his face into the narrow crack between door and frame, like a dog trying to nose open a door. "We heard this place was a safe haven." He dropped his voice to a conspiratorial whisper. "You know . . . for *travelers.*"

The female's face appeared below his. "Travelers from far away." She gave me a broad wink. "*Very* far away."

My weirdo radar, which I thought had been broken by overuse after hanging out at the B&B, was definitely buzzing now. Something was off.

"So...what, are you saying that you're not guests here?"

"Not as such."

"But we'd like to be."

"In fact, it's urgent—"

"Most urgent."

"—that we check in."

"Today."

"Right now."

This was too strange. Why hadn't they arrived in the transporters? I mean, I knew that spaceships existed, because I had seen a couple, but they didn't visit often. And I'd never seen an alien just show up at the front door.

But wait—Grandma had been running this place for forty years—there were probably lots of things I'd never seen before. What to do?

"How did you get here?"

They glanced at each other, the male looking straight down, the female straight up. Finally they faced me again. The male cleared his throat. "We're sorry, it's just that—"

"We're not in the habit of trusting, you know, *humans*. No offense intended, you understand."

Whatever. "Look, you're the ones who came here, remember? I can shut the door if you'd rather—"

"No!"

"Then how did you get here?" I repeated.

"Well...that's kind of a long story," the male said.

"Oh, it is not," the female said. "Our, uh, *vehicle* crashed. There, that's a pretty short story."

The male winced. "It's a little embarrassing."

"I should say so." The female huffed. "Some people don't know how to read a simple navigational chart, or even how to—"

"Someone's coming!" the male said.

I looked down the street. A group of kids were riding their bikes in this direction. Time to act.

"Go around the side of the house. Meet me on the back porch."

I shut the door and marched down the hallway, my mind racing. What was I supposed to do? I couldn't let aliens into the house if they didn't even have a reservation, could I? I mean, there must be some kind of off-world screening process for anyone who wanted to use a transporter. The last aliens that had shown up by ship without authorization hadn't been too friendly. They had, in fact, tried to kidnap pretty much the entire town of Forest Grove.

But, okay, these two didn't seem very intimidating. And it's not like I wanted them to just stroll into town, either. I had to get this figured out. Fast.

I couldn't believe how often I was thinking it, but I really wished the adults were back. Responsibility is overrated.

I opened the back door to find the aliens in the yard, craning their necks to study the windows on the top floors. Shutting the door firmly behind me, I stepped out onto the porch.

It took the male only a few long-legged steps to climb the porch stairs. "I'll get right down to business, as you earthlings like to say: We need a place to stay while we fix our ship. It's in the forest, about a half mile from here."

The little female bustled up behind him. They must have come from a planet with no concept of personal space, because they both crowded me. I stepped back, but the female leaned in even closer.

"We covered it with tree branches. Wouldn't want anyone —any *earthlings*—to find the ship, now, would we?" she said, her voice thick with implications. "It would be a shame if the authorities suspected it belonged here . . . *wouldn't* it?"

An alarm sounded somewhere in my brain. You know that parent trick, where they pretend to know way more about something than they actually do, and they start casually talking to you about it, and pretty soon you're accidentally giving up new details? That was definitely the vibe I was getting here.

As any kid knows, the only thing to do is play dumb and try to see where the adults are going with it.

"Why would anyone suspect that?" I didn't look directly at the female's eyes. Maybe she had some sort of alien-hypnosis power. You never know.

The male scanned Grandma's big backyard. "Speaking of ships, where are they all parked, anyway?"

"The ships?" I said.

"You know . . . for the *travelers* . . . ?" the male said, elbowing me gently, letting me know that we were two good buddies sharing the same big secret. "The ones out front are just decoration. We checked."

"The real ones must be hidden somewhere," the female said.

"Of course." The male nodded in approval. "Can't be too careful."

"Underground storage?" The female's orange eyebrows were raised in a question at me.

Hold on... They didn't know about the transporters? This was too bizarre. How was it even possible for two aliens to not know—?

Wait a minute.

It *wasn't* possible for two aliens to not know about the transporters.

I reached out and ran my finger along the female's forearm. She gasped. The tip of my finger came away smudged with orange makeup.

"How rude! You have no right to—"

I ignored her and grabbed the male's round nose. It popped right off his face. He staggered backward, covering up his very human nose with both hands. I tossed the yellow rubber schnoz back at him.

It all clicked into place. "You're the couple who tried to take pictures on the Fourth of July!" I said. "With the blue skin? Trying to get in here afterward? I found one of your rubber ears when you ran off."

The female smacked the tall one. "I told you these get-ups wouldn't work." Her voice had changed, dropped a few octaves. She had been doing an impersonation of what she thought an alien sounded like.

I narrowed my eyes. "You've been watching the house, haven't you? The hot air balloon? The car down the street? Why don't you just leave us alone?"

The male held up both hands, palms out: *I come in peace.* "Okay, kid, look. We can explain everything." The pinkish hue of his real nose made it stand out comically against the yellow alien makeup all over his face.

"We're on your side," the female said.

"One hundred percent." The male nodded eagerly. "We promise."

"What do you mean, my side?" Time to go into full denial mode. "There are no *sides*. We're running a bed-and-breakfast with an outer-space theme. Looks like you two got a little carried away with the whole idea."

They exchanged a meaningful glance. The male cleared his throat. "Well...we don't think that's exactly true."

"There's something else going on here," the female said.

I shrugged. "Think what you want." It was difficult to appear calm when my heart was beating so hard. This whole scene was really freaking me out. I couldn't decide which was worse: authentic shipwrecked aliens or nosy humans dressed up like aliens.

"We would just like to be allowed to come inside," the female said. "Check things out for ourselves."

"Too bad." I backed toward the door. "We're all booked up for the rest of the summer. But give us a call in a few months. Maybe we can squeeze you in for a quick stay this fall." I gestured toward their disguises. "Maybe around Halloween."

"Oh, we tried to make reservations, all right. We've been trying for over a year," the female said. "But we always seem to get turned down, or we get canceled due to lack of space, even in the off-season. Fishy business, young man. Very fishy, indeed."

The male kept his hands up where I could see them, his facial expression all innocence and good intentions, but he was slowly advancing across the porch. "If this is just an average bed-and-breakfast, kid, there should be no problem letting us in to look around."

I blurted out, "We reserve the right to refuse service." It was lame, but it was the only thing I could think of. The doorknob pressed into the small of my back. There was nowhere else to run. The yellow man kept advancing. "Stop right there," I warned, "or I'll call the police."

"The police?"

"That's right. I don't know about dressing up like freaks, but spying has to be against the law."

The man froze. Good.

But then he looked at the woman. And they both chuckled.

Not good.

"Okay," he said.

"Okay, what?"

He shrugged. "Okay, call the police."

"We'll wait right here," the female said.

How could they be so confident about calling my bluff? Who *were* these people?

The door opened and I nearly fell over backward.

Cottage Cheese Head and the Blob tromped out onto the porch. They must have just come back from fishing, because they were still done up in their gear.

"These two giving you any trouble, David?"

It's always nice to have real aliens to save you from fake aliens. Especially when they looked like a couple of big, burly outdoor types.

"No. They were just leaving."

The strange couple backed away. The male put the false nose back on his face, as if that would allow him to preserve a little dignity.

"We'll be seeing you again, David," he said.

"Very soon," the woman added. Then they disappeared around the side of the house.

"What was that all about?" Cottage Cheese Head said.

I exhaled heavily. "They were humans."

The Blob snorted. "No kidding."

"Don't tell me those lame disguises actually fooled you for even a minute?" Cottage Cheese shook his head. "Well, what did they want?"

"I have no idea. Let's get back inside."

I shut the door behind us and walked into the kitchen. I needed a glass of water. And some quiet time to think. But they followed me.

"So . . ." said Cottage Cheese. "Is 'fishing' an actual human recreational activity, or were you pulling a prank on us? Because basically we just stood around all afternoon, feeding worms to the river."

"Not the most thrilling three hours of my life," said the Blob.

I nodded. "Yep, that's fishing."

"Earthlings are weird," said Cottage Cheese Head.

"That's what I hear." I needed some time alone, to plan how I was going to handle those two people. "Look, guys, I'm going to go upstairs and—"

Whoa. The Blob's clothes suddenly puffed up like an inflatable toy. His flannel shirt stretched out, seams taut, until pink jelly-bubbles pooched out between the buttons. Then the buttons popped right off. His Levi's split down the sides and sloughed off his expanding body. Pretty soon he was back to himself, a big heap of pink blobbiness surrounded by ripped-up clothes.

"Looks like you made it back inside just in time," Cottage Cheese Head said. They both laughed.

But it made me realize how close those two humans had come to getting inside the house and witnessing something like that. Why had they come? They didn't act angry or scared, like the mob of townsfolk that had converged on the B&B last summer. Instead, they seemed... *eager*.

And maybe that was worse.

I was pacing on the front porch, thinking about the costumed humans—What did they want? How much did they know?—when Amy returned with the alien class.

The kids raced down the walkway, chattering and shedding their human clothes. Mrs. Crowzen tottered along behind them, scooping up hats and tennis shoes.

"I'll be there in a second to make you a snack," Amy called as the kids rushed into the house. She climbed the steps and walked over to me. "Hey, there. We had fun but came back early because they're starving. I think we're going to—" She stopped, studying my face. "David? Is anything wrong?"

"I think we have trouble," I said. "Again."

"Oh, no." She clutched my arm. "Did my dad come home while everyone was out?"

I shook my head. "Worse."

I gave her the details about the weird humans, including their promise to come back. Soon.

"I knew it," she said. "Something just didn't feel right. We should have done more. We should have staked out that car and followed it back to wherever they're staying, or figured out how to—"

"Right, okay, but we can't worry about what we should've done." I shook my head, as if maybe that would clear it out and set the stage for a great idea. "We're the ones in charge, and we have to figure out what to do now."

"Hmmmmm." Amy chewed her lower lip. "If they tried to sneak in on the Fourth, that means they've been planning to get inside for a while. And if they've been monitoring the house, they probably know that you and I are here alone."

"You're not exactly helping me feel better."

"What do you think they want?"

"No idea."

Now she was the one pacing back and forth. I slumped down on Tate's driftwood bench, glad to have someone to share the worry with.

"I think we should go back into my dad's lockdown mode," she said. "I know it's lame, but it might be the only thing that works. Besides, the kids had their field trip, so Mrs. Crowzen shouldn't have anything to complain about."

"That's probably a good idea." I nodded. "Heck, we can just tell everybody to get into the transporters and go home.

Then lock the doors, close up the shutters, and hunker down. Wait for Grandma or your dad to get back."

Amy's face fell. "Oh, I guess that's probably best. But we should give them some coupons for a free weekend stay or something, to make up for it." She sighed, her shoulders slumping. "I just wanted the chance to show that we could do it—all by ourselves—you know? I imagined that your grandma would get back and everything would be running smoothly and she'd be so proud of us."

"She'll be proud of us if we keep those weirdoes out of her house."

"Yeah, I guess so." Amy stopped pacing and looked at me. "So we're agreed? Evacuation and lockdown, wait until the storm passes?"

I nodded.

"Where's my sister?" the bench said.

"AAAHHH!" Amy screamed and I yelled.

The shape of Kanduu became recognizable when he hopped off the bench. I swear, I'd never get used to that.

"What?" Amy said, when she had recovered.

"My sister. I thought she was with the girls, but they thought she was with me."

Amy and I looked at each other. "Wait a minute. Are you saying that—?"

Mrs. Crowzen stumbled out onto the porch, her face a mask of fear.

"One of the children is missing," she said.

When trouble comes to the B&B, it never comes alone. It always brings a few friends along for the ride.

I stood in front of a somber group of aliens, leading the discussion about little Kandeel. The last time anyone could remember seeing her was at the ice cream parlor, right in the middle of downtown Forest Grove. It had been the group's final stop after a tour of town. Apparently there was some confusion after a bathroom break, when the kids were supposed to form two groups for the walk home, and Kandeel had been left behind.

I said, "I wonder if there's any chance she'll come back on her own."

I had been thinking out loud, but Kanduu answered. "Negative. When she's scared, she hides. Totally freezes."

"And she's been scared pretty much the whole time we've been on this planet," Lizard Boy said.

Kanduu nodded. "She's never been off-world before. I bet she's already ditched those earthling clothes and is just blending in somewhere downtown."

"I don't think I'd be able to find the way back on my own," one of the girls added.

"Yeah," said another one. "Earth towns are pretty confusing. I didn't know that—"

"Okay, okay, I got it. She's not coming back on her own." I started pacing. "Moving on."

Amy sat hunched over on the couch, her head in her hands. "I'm sorry. I'm so, so sorry." It was approximately the 187th time she had said that.

"Amy, no one is blaming you, we just need to figure out how—"

"If I hadn't been so focused on telling them everything I knew about Forest Grove, none of this would have ever happened. It's all my fault."

"You?" Mrs. Crowzen wailed, clacking away with those claws. "What about me? A teacher's most important job on a field trip is to make sure her students are safe." She started leaking all over.

"Ladies, please. We can play the blame-and-shame game later, okay? Right now we need to figure out how to find

Kandeel." I scanned the crowd. Nobody was volunteering any ideas. I took a deep breath. "All right, let's look at the situation. The good news is that I'm sure none of the humans can see her. That girl is freaky good at hiding."

"That's also the bad news, though, right?" one of the former slime-drippers chimed in. "If she's impossible to see, how are we going to find her?"

I sighed heavily. "Yes, that's also the bad news." I paced some more. "Okay, look. How about this: Amy and I will go back into town, split up, and walk around. Keep our eyes open. We know Kandeel is scared, so if she sees us she's likely to say something, do something to get our attention. Right? Then we can sort of smuggle her back here. She's tiny. Think that'll work?"

Everyone shook their heads no.

"Why not?"

Nobody had a plan, but everybody had an opinion about mine.

"—because she's kind of scared of you, too, and—"

"—voice is so quiet, you'll never hear her downtown with all of the—"

"—sure, the town's small, but still too big for just two people to get around to all of—"

"—what if someone sees her without her disguise when you pick her up and—"

Snarffle whistle-whined along with the nervous babble.

I held up my hands for silence.

"Okay, okay. I got it. That plan won't work." More pacing. "Moving on."

"And besides," Kanduu said, "we do not have the necessary time to complete this already impossible task."

"What do you mean?" I said. "There's no time limit. We just have to keep thinking until we come up with a good plan, and then search until we find her."

Kanduu shook his head again. "Remember the beacon? From the night of the sky show?"

Oh, crap. "Everybody in Forest Grove remembers that beacon," I said. And they wouldn't think it was part of the fireworks display this time.

"When she gets scared enough, she'll use it," Kanduu said. "We definitely have a time limit."

Mrs. Crowzen started wailing again.

"Please," I said. "This isn't helping. We need to—"

"You don't understand." She sniveled noisily. "I send a report each evening to the school. When I say that one of the children is missing, the parents will be notified immediately, and—"

"Oh, no," Kanduu said.

"What?"

"I told you my mom's overprotective. Once she hears that, she'll be here straightaway. And she won't care about any secret you earthlings are trying to keep, either. She'll stomp into town and tear the place apart until she gets Kandeel back."

"That would probably not look real good on the front page of the *Forest Grove Gazette*," the Blob said.

"Thanks for the advice," I said. Although, to be honest, keeping Grandma's secret was not the first thing on my mind right at that moment. It was the safety of that little girl. She must be terrified. And what if someone else found her? Where would they take her? What would they do to her?

I couldn't let it happen.

"Look, this isn't helping. We need to think up a workable plan."

"Soon." Kanduu nodded his little head. "Now."

Amy straightened up, pulled herself together a little bit. "Okay. Instead of talking about what won't work, let's talk about what *will* work. Anybody? Anything?"

The crowd was silent for a moment, deep in thought.

"Well..." Mrs. Crowzen finally said, "... if she saw us—the *real* us, that is, without our disguises—she would most likely feel comfortable enough to come out of hiding. Rejoin us."

Amy rolled her eyes at me in exasperation, but she patted Mrs. Crowzen on the back of her shell and nodded patiently. "Okay... it's good to start a brainstorming session by throwing out any idea that pops up. But we don't have much time. Does anybody have anything that we could actually do?"

As I looked at the crowd of aliens, an image popped into my head: the faces of all the Tourists sitting around the kitchen table when the famous Evanblatt Snappyfalls came in with his entourage of broadcasting Mailboxes. Their awed expressions and goofy grins, the waving, the hushed excitement. The temporary abandonment of reason and common sense, basically.

And just like that, I had a plan.

I pointed at Mrs. Crowzen. "That's actually really good. We can use it."

"Use what?" Amy said. "How can her idea help us? We can't just stroll down Main Street with a parade of undisguised alien Tourists."

I shrugged. "Why not?"

Strolling down Main Street with a parade of undisguised alien Tourists was the most surreal thing I had experienced since starting to work at the Intergalactic Bed & Breakfast.

And that's saying something.

We weren't downtown yet, but the residential neighborhood grew denser, and soon we were surrounded by houses. People peeked at us from behind curtains. Kids dropped their toys and stared wide-eyed from their front yards. The Emergency Canine Broadcast System went on full alert, with every dog on the block barking to announce our arrival.

"I hope you know what you're doing," Amy whispered.

I swallowed. "Me too."

Snarffle strained at his leash, eager to say hello to his furry earthbound cousins yapping away behind fences. I did not want to find out what would happen if one of those dogs gave Snarffle a butt-sniffing Earth greeting.

"Make sure you keep a strong grip on his leash," I told Cottage Cheese Head.

I tugged on the red Radio Flyer wagon and surveyed the rest of our entourage. "And can you all tone down the jumps a little bit?" I called to the Arkamendian Air Painters. "Dancing is okay, but nobody on this planet can actually hang in the air that long. There, that's better. But—come on, ladies—no rainbows. No, not even little ones. We discussed this."

Mrs. Crowzen's big round shell glowed pink in the sunlight, and her claws clicked along the asphalt. As one of the most exotic-looking Tourists, she was drawing lots of stares and pointed fingers from the townsfolk. "I've never been out in the open like this on a primitive planet before," she said, scanning the rows of surrounding houses. "I feel so exposed."

Well, it was pretty much your idea. "Don't worry," I said. "Just remember: this is all for Kandeel. As soon as we find her we'll get everyone safely back inside. I promise."

The Pink Blob was the other Tourist getting the most attention as he slithered down the middle of the road. I sidled up to him. "Hey. Can you, like, move a little more awkwardly?"

"What do you mean?"

"Your movements, they're too smooth. Fluid. Need to be a little more herky-jerky."

"Like this?" He sort of rocked his body stiffly side-to-side in a mocking imitation of a human lumbering around on two legs.

"Perfect." Well, not perfect. But better.

The Blob smiled. "I'll just pretend I'm Mr. Security Man Tate." Then he scowled, pooched out his blobby belly, and made his movements even more rigid.

Even Amy, nervous as she was, smiled at that one.

I looked at the kids. They were all over the place, reveling in their new freedom. Jumping off the curbs, kicking pebbles, teasing and shoving each other. Just like Earth kids, basically. I didn't give them any further instruction.

The closer we got to downtown with our colorful parade, the more nervous I became. What we were doing went against all of my B&B training, betrayed every one of my instincts. I tried to breathe deeply, calm myself down, but my chest still grew tight, and it felt like I wasn't getting quite enough oxygen.

Man, I hope this works, I thought. At least I could take comfort in the fact that if it totally failed, Kandeel would set off the beacon, then Mrs. Crowzen would report her missing, and her mom would show up and storm into town. Either way, the end result would be the same: complete catastrophe.

"Here they come," Amy said, pointing. "You were right, David. Someone must have called from one of the houses."

A sheriff's patrol vehicle and a black town car were creeping down the road. Headed right for us.

More deep breaths. I could do this. We could do this.

"All part of the plan," I said.

"I really hope you know what you're doing."

"Yeah. You mentioned that."

17

The cars stopped a good twenty yards away from our other-worldly posse.

"Okay, everybody, form up, just like we talked about." The kids circled Mrs. Crowzen; the Air Painters huddled together; and Cottage Cheese Head, the Blob, and Snarffle positioned themselves in the lead. "And let me do the talking." I stepped in front of the group, pulling the little red wagon behind me.

Sheriff Tisdall—Tate's former deputy from his law enforcement days—stepped out of the patrol vehicle, his ratlike features twisted into a sneer. Then the mayor of Forest Grove emerged from a town car. She was dressed in a conservative suit, all one drab color.

"I'll handle this," she said to Tisdall. She took a couple of businesslike steps forward, stopped, and looked over the gaggle of aliens. Then she called over her shoulder, "But stay close."

Tisdall lifted a finger to the brim of his hat and sat on the hood of the patrol car, one foot on the bumper. He never took his squinty eyes off the Tourists, or his hand off his gun belt.

"Hi, Mrs. Mayor." I tried to sound as cheerful as possible. I extended my hand, but she didn't take it. "We're from the Intergalactic Bed and Breakfast."

"I gathered that." She took her eyes off the aliens for a moment to study me. "And I remember you, as well. Caused quite a stir last summer, if memory serves. Apparently there were rumors concerning guests at your establishment. Guests that were perhaps...rather unusual?" She inclined her head toward the off-world visitors hanging out in the middle of the road.

"Yeah." I shook my head and forced out a chuckle. I hoped it didn't sound as fake as it felt. "Some people actually thought we had space aliens staying at the b-and-b. *Real* ones." I raised my eyebrows and made a *Small-town-people-say-the-darndest-things* face. "Can you believe that?"

The mayor let her eyes drift over the Tourists again. "Yes." She took a small step backward. Then a bigger one. "Yes, I can."

People started creeping out of their homes, lining up along fences, watching the show. I could tell the mayor was aware of the growing crowd—her eyes flicked to the side, taking in the townsfolk with her peripheral vision—but she kept most of her attention on the aliens.

She had been taken by surprise, obviously, and didn't know what to do. Didn't even know if she could trust her own eyes. This is what I was counting on.

"Well"—I picked up the wagon's handle again—"we're heading into town now."

"I'm afraid I can't let you do that," the mayor said. Behind her, Tisdall slid off the car and straightened up, ready for action.

"Why not?" I tried to sound as innocent as possible.

"Well, your guests are... that is to say, I can't exactly..." She gestured vaguely at the Tourists, a mixture of curiosity and fear on her face. "I need to vouch for the safety... that is, the well-being of every citizen...."

She was really struggling to spit out what she wanted to say. Situations like this were probably not covered in the *Total Idiot's Guide to Being a Small-Town Mayor.* I was counting on that, too.

"The safety of the citizens? Really?" I shook my head sadly. "Mrs. Mayor, you're not saying that you actually believe those crazy outer space rumors." I let that sink in for a few moments, made sure she fully realized that everyone would hear her answer. "Are you?"

The mayor studied the Tourists, particularly the Pink Blob. He smiled and waved at her. She shuddered a little bit.

"Are you saying these are not... I mean, that they're just wearing...?"

"Costumes. Of course. What—did you think I was walking into town with a bunch of real space creatures?" I inserted another fake chuckle here. "No disrespect intended, Mrs. Mayor, but when I say something like that, my mom tells me I've been watching too many movies."

The mayor glanced at the crowd again. Where I only saw curious people, she must have seen skeptical constituents. She cleared her throat and stood up straighter, her face making it clear that she had come to some kind of decision.

"I'm sorry. I'm not going to be able to let you all go into town."

"Why not?"

"These . . . costumes. They're too realistic. It's downright unsettling. Could cause a public disturbance."

I turned to the aliens. "You hear that? Great job on the costumes, everybody! Our masquerade party is going to be the best ever this year."

"What does unsettling mean?" said Lizard Boy.

"It means you look great! Just like a real alien."

The Tourists grinned and high-fived and really played it up. The Pink Blob raised his stumpy arms in celebration and shook, his body jiggling all over. The Air Painters linked arms and danced in a circle, fuzz floating through the air. Mrs. Crowzen clacked her claws and turned this way and that, the sun glinting off her plates.

"See?" I said to the mayor. "It's all in good fun. We'd really like to go into town now, if you don't mind."

She shook her head. "No. It would be more than a little unnerving for the citizens and would disturb the peace, at the very least. Surely you remember the angry mob that descended upon the bed-and-breakfast last summer?" She gave me a pointed look. "Nothing of the kind will happen on my watch again. In fact, we may need to send Sheriff Tisdall and his colleagues down to search the bed-and-breakfast after a stunt like this. It is my sworn duty to look out for the best interests of Forest Grove, and I take that very seriously."

Perfect. Time to unleash the secret weapons.

I hunched over the red wagon and lifted the blanket that was hiding the cargo. Tisdall stepped forward, his hand moving to the butt of his gun, but he relaxed when he saw what was in the wagon.

"Actually, I think our plan is very much in the best interests of Forest Grove." I lifted one of Tate's clunky surveillance cameras and handed it to Amy. Then I hoisted the other one onto my shoulder. "We're going to make a commercial. To drum up business for sci-fi fans that might want to stay at the bed-and-breakfast, you know? But I was thinking it could actually be more of an advertisement for the town of Forest Grove itself."

"A commercial?" The mayor blinked a few times. "For Forest Grove?"

"Yeah." Amy stepped forward, adjusting the lens. The mayor got that Bambi-in-the-headlights look that hits people when they suddenly realize they're on camera. "To show people that Forest Grove is welcoming to the science-fiction enthusiast." She gestured at our alien guests. "There are a lot of them out there, you know."

"Ever seen how many people show up in full costume to those *Star Trek* conventions? Or Comic-Con?" I said. "Thousands."

"Tens of thousands," Amy continued. "And the people

who end up coming here will spend lots of money at shops and restaurants."

"We plan on filming at different locations around town, showcasing as many local businesses as possible. Should be a real boost for tourism around here." I dropped my voice so only the mayor could hear. "You probably wouldn't mind *that* happening on your watch."

The mayor cleared her throat, glanced at the ground for a moment. "Well... I don't know... this is all very sudden...."

I looked at the crowd again. I recognized a guy leaning over the fence in the next yard. "Hey, Mr. McClure. You're the owner of Outdoor Adventures downtown, right? You guys run river-rafting tours on the Nooksack?"

He looked startled to be singled out of the crowd. But he quickly recovered. "Yeah. That's me."

"Well, this commercial we're making will run all over Washington State, including Seattle. Lots of people in that city need a getaway, for sure. Hundreds of thousands of potential customers will see this ad. Maybe a million." I pointed the camera at him. "What do you think—would you mind if we mentioned your business? Maybe got a shot of one of the Intergalactic Bed and Breakfast 'aliens' here with one of your rafts?"

"Huh. Never had the budget for a fancy TV commercial before." Mr. McClure looked around at his neighbors, then finally nodded. "Sure. That just might be good for business. You all go ahead and stop by."

"And, Mrs. Vaughn," Amy called to a woman across the street. "You run the Forest Grove Bakery, yes? Maybe we could get footage of our customers enjoying your pastries. We could make them famous all over the state!"

"And have you ever seen those crazy commercials that go viral on the Internet?" I said. "Forget the state; you could be famous all over the *world*."

"Oooohh, *famous*? Really?" When Amy swung the camera in her direction, Mrs. Vaughn smoothed out her frumpy housedress. "You don't say. Well, yes, I would like that. Have to change first, though. Freshen up a bit." She giggled like a nervous little girl.

"Of course," Amy said.

"Well"—I looked back at the mayor—"how about it?"

She still looked unsure, although I knew she must have been feeling the tide turning among all of those taxpaying registered voters. "I'm not entirely certain of the protocol. I think you probably need a permit for something like that...?"

"Good point. That's why we were going to stop by your office first." *Time to go for the kill.* "In fact, we decided that it would be best if you were actually in the commercial. The Voice of Forest Grove. We could film you taking our customers on a guided tour around town."

"It would convey that personal touch we're going for in this ad," Amy said. "You know, the homey hospitality folks can find here. Even the most out-of-town tourists"—she swept her hand toward our colorful entourage—"are welcome in Forest Grove. You'd be the perfect person to illustrate that message."

A flush crept across the mayor's cheeks. "I've only ever been on cable access TV, when they broadcast the city council meetings." She lifted her fingers absentmindedly to her hair, fluffing it up, putting it into place. "I've never been in a bona fide commercial before...."

"Don't worry. You'll be great," I said.

The faint trace of a smile played on the mayor's lips. "So I would be a spokesperson of sorts? For the whole town?"

"Exactly," I said.

"Actually," Amy chimed in, "more like an actress. Or a model."

"Oh, my. A model? I don't think..." The mayor fumbled with one of the buttons on her jacket, then pulled down on its bottom hem, straightening out the creases. I fiddled with the lens on my camera, tilting it this way and that, as if I were trying to get the best angle on her. "That is to say, I've never—"

"Can I be in your commercial too?" someone shouted from a nearby yard.

"What about us?" yelled a kid.

"We can do skateboard tricks!" one of his friends added.

"I own the hardware store," another called. "We could get hard hats and power tools for your friends there, be a great shot for your commercial. Right beside the sign, out in front of the store."

The Pink Blob sidled up to me. "I think it's working," he whispered out of the side of his mouth.

"Yeah," I said. "Earthlings tend to temporarily lose their minds when you point a TV camera at them."

The Blob chuckled. "I noticed."

I looked over at Kanduu. "You can write that one down and put it in your report," I whispered.

Amy called to the crowd, "We'll try to get as many people in the commercial as we can, I promise."

I turned back to the mayor. "So how about it? Think you might be able to speed up that permit process for us?"

"Oh, who needs to fuss with a lot of paperwork," the mayor said brightly. "I'd be happy to give you a guided tour of Forest Grove for your big commercial!"

18

If you ever take a group of space aliens on a public outing, I recommend bringing a camera crew, police escort, mayoral presence, and crowd of onlookers.

Grandma once told me that she used the outer space theme so that her business could "hide out in the open." As I filmed the Pink Blob giving squishy high-fives to kids lining the edge of the street, I realized that it didn't get any more open than this.

Word of our arrival preceded us. As we entered the core of downtown, business owners and customers alike came out to watch from the sidewalk. The mayor snapped into administrator mode, clearing a path through the onlookers and enthusiastically explaining the benefits of our commercial to anyone who would listen. She kept calling it "our gift to Forest Grove."

It really was like a parade. If Kandeel was anywhere around here, she was going to see us.

And the magic of the cameras continued to work wherever we pointed them.

Everyone wanted to be in our commercial. The townsfolk all had eyes for that little red recording light, no doubt more concerned with how they were going to look on TV than with any aliens.

The mayor also helped to set up our shots. We stopped outside the barbershop, where Mr. Gill posed with a big smile and his scissors, pretending to trim up the antennae sprouting out of the kids' heads for an "alien haircut."

The woman who taught dance-aerobics classes at the local gym rounded up some extra headbands and leggings for the Air Painters. We filmed a nice scene of the fuzzy aliens as they gracefully flitted around a group of sweaty grown-ups to techno music.

The little old ladies who ran Sew and Sew, the fabric and knitting supply place, brought out several of their homemade creations—shawls and hats and blankets—and draped them all over Mrs. Crowzen. She obliged them by strutting in front of the camera, turning this way and that to show off the knitted goods. She seemed to enjoy the spotlight as much as the humans.

While we filmed our "commercial," Sheriff Tisdall was

always on the outer perimeter of the action, monitoring the proceedings through scowling eyes.

Hopefully we would spot Kandeel before he did. As we pointed the cameras at the festivities, Amy and I constantly scanned the surrounding buildings. The little girl alien had to be somewhere close.

"I can't believe this is working," I whispered.

"It's not over yet," Amy answered. "We still need to actually find her."

"There's no way she can miss all of this commotion. She'll find us."

Our tour around town continued. At one point we passed in front of a big Victorian house with a sign announcing that it was Miss Kitty's Bed and Breakfast. It was pretty weird to see the tasteful paint job and the crowd of guests politely watching from the front porch. Human guests. Man, how boring.

We also came upon the group of old-timers who sat outside Dunlop's Diner every day. They all still wore the classic lumberjack combo of jeans and flannel shirts and suspenders even though their working days in the woods were decades in the past. From what I could tell, their main daily activity was sipping coffee while arguing about the upcoming season of Forest Grove High football.

They elbowed each other as we walked by, and there was lots of head shaking and smirking.

"Would you take a look at this, Jed?"

"Those are some pretty outlandish duds those folks got on there."

"Not something you see every day."

"Not something you'd *want* to see every day."

"Leastways not in Forest Grove."

One of the old-timers leaned over the railing and poked at where the Blob's shoulders would be if the Blob had shoulders. "Just where you folks from, anyhow?"

The Blob glanced at me. I nodded, hoping he'd remember the answer we rehearsed.

"New York City."

The group exploded with guffaws and knee slaps.

"Haw!"

"That explains it, all right."

"Edna tried to get me to take her all the way out there once." Jed cocked one bushy gray eyebrow and studied the aliens. "Glad I said no."

The mayor whisked us away from Dunlop's. "Don't pay them any mind," she muttered.

But nothing could dampen the festive air downtown. We jumped at the offer from the owner of the Big Scoop ice cream parlor to film an impromptu sundae-eating competition, since it was the last place anyone could remember seeing Kandeel. And even though they'd had ice cream earlier in the day, the kids shoveled it in, hot fudge dripping down their scaly faces while the crowd cheered them on. Just a slice of small-town Americana. Plus, you know, aliens.

But I still didn't see Kandeel anywhere, no matter how carefully I examined the brickwork along the buildings or the wood grain of the sidewalk benches, looking for the slightest hint of movement.

We continued filming all over town, including stops at the bookstore, auto body shop, and beauty salon. Mrs. Crowzen ended up with a much better makeup job than her clown mask. But she was still minus one student.

I was starting to feel extremely uneasy. I had been so focused on pulling off the undisguised alien parade that I hadn't thought about what would happen if we weren't successful in finding our missing Tourist. As usual, I didn't have a Plan B.

Our last possible stop was in front of the toy store, pretty much the only business that hadn't been filmed yet. By this time we had enough footage for a three-hour documentary on Forest Grove.

I was barely even pretending to look through the viewfinder anymore. I pointed the camera in the general direction of the hula hoop contest the toy shop owner had set up for the aliens while I scanned the surrounding area. I made sure to search the upper floors of the downtown buildings; Kandeel might have blended in and climbed up there, where she could look down at the strange town and maybe feel a little more safe.

So it took me completely by surprise when Amy elbowed me and whispered, "There she is."

"Where?" My eyes darted all over the block.

"There!"

Turns out I should have been looking through the camera lens after all, because Amy pointed right where we were filming. Sure enough, there was Kandeel, clutching her brother inside one of the rotating hula hoops.

"How did she get there?"

"No idea. But as you said yourself—she is freaky good at hiding."

"However she pulled it off, it's definitely time to get out of here." I stepped in front of the hula-hooping space creatures and addressed the crowd. "Thank you so much for everything, Forest Grove. We're going to head back to the b-and-b now. We sure appreciate all your hospitality."

The crowd groaned.

"But you didn't get any footage around City Hall."

"How about the library?"

"Or the farmers' market?"

I raised my hand for silence. "I think we have all the shots we need, and then some. It's going to be a great commercial. I'm really looking forward to seeing you all get famous." That got some laughs and a few cheers.

While I talked to the crowd, Amy rounded up the Tourists, herding them toward the road that would lead us back to Grandma's.

The aliens made the most of their red carpet treatment, waving to the crowd and shaking hands along the way.

As we started to make our way out of the crush of people —with our mission accomplished and the finish line nearly in sight—my nerves caught up with me all at once. I had been so amped up to pull this off that the adrenaline must have kept away the nervousness. Now that it looked like we were going to get out of this safely, my body was going through a delayed reaction—shaky legs, sweaty palms, the whole deal. I just tried to look straight ahead and keep walking to calm down. We'd be home in a few minutes.

The crowd was fairly quiet as we were leaving, so Sheriff Tisdall's voice really carried when he said, "Just what is that *dog* doing to those flowers?"

19

Every head in the crowd turned to look where Deputy Tisdall was pointing.

Cottage Cheese Head was blowing kisses to his new earthling admirers while Snarffle's leash trailed from his other hand. The little purple alien was chomping away on a bush of rhododendrons that lined the sidewalk, his tail spinning like a propeller. Yikes. With everything going on, I had forgotten to give him his third before-dinner snack, and rhododendrons were one of his favorites.

Not good.

"Whoops. Sorry about that." I grinned sheepishly at the

mayor. "Must be feeding time. We'll run him back to the b-and-b and get some dinner into him. But we can pay for the flowers."

"Oh, don't worry." She tapped the camera on my shoulder. "The town can always use some of those new tourism dollars to buy another rhodie bush."

"That's not what I meant." Tisdall sauntered through the crowd into the middle of our little clearing. He sneered at me and then looked at the mayor. "I'm not overly worried about the flowers in this town. They're not exactly a matter of public safety."

"Then what, exactly, is your point, sir?" the mayor said.

"My point"—he jerked his thumb at Snarffle—"is that dogs don't eat flowers."

The mayor and I, along with everyone else in town, examined Snarffle. He grinned and wagged his long tongue, happy to be the center of attention. A clump of pinkish-white petals stuck to the slobber on his cheeks.

"Especially not that many," continued Tisdall.

Indeed, half the bush was already gone.

"That *is* rather unusual . . ." said the mayor.

"Now, I might believe that you could take a dog and dress him up in a little outfit." Tisdall turned to look at me, but you could tell by his voice that he was really addressing the entire crowd. "But I don't buy that a dog—a *real* one, mind you—would be eating a bunch of flowers like that."

I stepped forward. "We've been meaning to take him to obedience school, but just haven't found the time to—"

"I'm not finished."

Tisdall sauntered by the outer space lineup and stopped

in front of the Pink Blob. "What's this material made of, anyway? Never seen anything like it." Tisdall reached out and squeezed a handful of the alien's belly, the jellylike skin making a squelching sound as it oozed between the deputy's fingers. The Blob threw up his stumpy arms and giggled hysterically.

"Stop it!" he cried. "That tickles!"

Tisdall arched one eyebrow and looked at the crowd. "Your *costume* is ticklish? How's that work?"

He let go of the Blob and pointed at one of the little girl aliens. "And just what is going on over there?"

All eyes turned toward her. She had kept one of the hula hoops, but instead of swiveling her hips to rotate it around her body, human-style, she was using a different technique. Her feet and head remained stationary while her entire torso spun around and around in complete circles, keeping the hoop aloft.

I had no idea she could do that. I gave her a few quick head shakes that I hoped no one else noticed.

The girl alien winced sheepishly and quit moving. The hula hoop clattered to her feet.

But she had stopped with her torso facing the wrong way, her arms sticking out behind her where her back should be. I caught her eye and made a little spinning motion with my index finger, and she slowly rotated her body back into position.

Tisdall just shook his head and took a long look at the rest of the aliens, inviting the townsfolk to do the same. "These are some mighty realistic costumes, all right; almost like something from a big-time Hollywood movie." He faced me again, but his words were clearly still meant for the crowd. "Seems like you have quite the impressive budget for your little commercial here. Guess you must be charging a pretty penny for your rooms. Is *that* the reason why I've heard it's so hard to get a reservation up there? Or is something else going on?"

The expressions on the people around us clouded a bit. They hadn't turned against us yet, not by a long shot, but you could tell that Tisdall was giving them something to think about.

Time to get out. Now. "Sorry again about the flowers, Mrs. Mayor. We need to be getting back." I tried to usher out the aliens, but Tisdall stepped forward and placed his hand against my chest to stop me.

"After all the money you spent, you must be pretty proud of these costumes here." He gestured toward Mrs. Crowzen, who suddenly looked very afraid. "I'm sure you wouldn't mind if we inspect them a little more closely, see just how you pulled this off."

He took a step toward Mrs. Crowzen. She shrank back a bit, but was already pressed up against the wall of people. There was nowhere for her to go. Tisdall reached out his hand to grab at her.

Oh, no. No, no, no.

"Let's just see if we can't lift one of these shells off and check what's under—"

"Wait a minute!" a voice cried.

A couple pushed their way through the crowd and into the little clearing. They were wearing silvery jumpsuits. The tall one had yellow skin, spiky hair, and an enormous nose. The little one had more of an orangey tint and a beehive hairdo that reached for the stars.

"So sorry we're late," the female said.

"And just who—or *what*—are you supposed to be?" Tisdall glowered at the newcomers.

"Well, I thought that was pretty obvious, especially for you." The little one spread out her arms to indicate her out-landish costume. "We're aliens from outer space, of course. Just like all of these creatures. Looks like you really blew this case wide open, officer."

That drew some nervous laughter from the crowd and a glare from Tisdall.

"Please forgive my wife," Tall-and-Yellow said. "She's just

upset because we missed out on being in the big commercial. We are guests, of course, at the Intergalactic Bed and Breakfast." He extended his hand, but Tisdall ignored it.

"We booked our reservations after some friends of ours raved about the b-and-b," the female said.

"And about Forest Grove," her partner added.

"Yes, that's right. We're just the sort of folks that will be targeted in this commercial." She turned to the mayor. "And yes, we will be spreading our discretionary income around your fine town."

That got a smattering of applause from the citizens of Forest Grove.

"So if you want to start inspecting some costumes, maybe you should start with us." Tall-and-Yellow turned to the crowd, approached a young girl holding hands with her dad, and bent down until he was face-to-face with her. "Why don't you tug on that big nose of mine a little bit?"

The girl looked up at her dad, who nodded his permission. The nose popped right off the tall man's face. "Now, you tell me, does that look like a real alien nose?" The girl squished the rubbery schnoz between her fingers, then giggled and shook her head. "No. I didn't think so," the man said.

He turned, scanned the crowd, and found a little boy. "The sheriff here wants an inspection. Why don't you check out this hair of mine. Give it a pull."

The boy reached up and snatched the spiky wig right off, revealing the man's bald head underneath. "That doesn't look like alien hair, does it?" The boy grinned and shook his head.

"Although maybe I really am an alien." The man straightened up and rubbed his baldness. "Human heads aren't supposed to be this shiny, are they?" That got a big laugh from the crowd.

I was speechless as I watched along with the rest of Forest Grove. *Who were these people?* The mystery only deepened. Wherever they'd come from, the couple had totally defused the tension that Tisdall had built just a few moments earlier.

The man turned to Tisdall and started to peel off the shiny silver jumpsuit he was wearing. "So . . . should I just take everything off, Mr. Sheriff? Right here in front of everyone?"

"That won't be necessary," said the mayor.

Mrs. Crowzen stepped forward. "And I'm afraid that my costume is not available for inspection."

Tisdall grunted. "Why's that?"

"Well . . . it's a warm summer day." Mrs. Crowzen cleared her throat. "I'm not exactly wearing anything under these shells."

More crowd reaction at that, chuckles and murmurs and people calling out to the officer.

"Oh, leave 'em alone, Tisdall."

"Yeah, they're just having a little fun."

Amy sidled up to the lawman and whispered, "Remember what happened to the last law enforcement officer who made a bunch of crazy claims about aliens in town? He no longer works for Forest Grove."

"Yeah, your dad works for you kooks now," Tisdall said between gritted teeth.

"Exactly. And we're not hiring at the moment." Amy

smiled sweetly. "So you better be careful about what happens next."

I took that as my cue. I spoke up, loud enough for everyone to hear. "It's been a long day, and we have lots of editing ahead of us so we can get this commercial on the air before the summer tourist season is over. What do you say, Officer Tisdall? Can we go now?"

What other choice did he possibly have? With one last glare at Amy and me, he turned and stormed back to his patrol car.

We quickly herded the Tourists down the street, everyone smiling and waving good-bye to the surrounding humans.

The silver-jumpsuited couple followed us, part of our group now. Because what other choice did we possibly have?

· ✺ ·

We marched out of town and through the residential neighborhoods until we were back on the quiet, tree-lined road that led to the Intergalactic Bed & Breakfast. After being cooped up in the house for so long, the day of adventure and danger and way too much ice cream had left the kids exhausted. Their antennae drooped and various appendages dragged along the road.

Amy led the whole group while I lagged behind with the mystery couple.

When the last person from town was well behind us, I turned and spoke to them, keeping my voice low. "You two still aren't getting into the bed-and-breakfast."

"After that scene downtown, I think you owe us a little more hospitality than that," the woman said. "Maybe we could come in for just a quick cup of tea."

"No way."

"There's no need to be afraid," said the man, fixing the spiky wig back in place on top of his head. "We told you— we're on your side."

"We're nothing like that horrible, narrow-minded lawman back there."

"Please. All we're asking is for ten minutes of your time," the man said. "Fifteen, tops."

I took a deep breath. I wasn't sure how much I owed them …but with Amy and me in charge all by ourselves, it was probably a good idea to know something about these people, learn what they wanted and why they kept trying to crash the place dressed up like aliens.

"Okay, but not at the b-and-b. Tomorrow morning. Nine a.m. Riverside Park. Meet me by the picnic tables." That was a nice open area with clear sightlines all around. They wouldn't be able to try anything too weird out there. "I'll give you your ten minutes."

I thought they would protest, but both of their faces lit up with big smiles. "Oh, thank you."

"Until then, go back to wherever you're actually staying." I stopped walking and looked them up and down, from their crazy wigs and painted faces to their shiny silver go-go boots. "Just do me a favor when we meet up tomorrow."

"Anything."

"Dress like humans for a change."

21

For the rest of the walk back to Grandma's I stared into the middle distance, lost in thought about my meeting with that weird couple tomorrow. So I was startled when something spongy pressed up against my palm.

I was doubly surprised when I looked down to see that it was Kandeel who had taken my hand. Her body turned the same color as my tanned skin. Aside from the antenna and segmented body rings, she could have passed for the little sister I never had.

"My brother told me it was your idea," she squeaked. "Thank you for coming to get me."

"You bet. But I should be the one thanking you for not setting off that beacon thing." I squeezed her hand a little bit. "That must have been hard. I'm sure it was scary to be in town by yourself."

She nodded. "But it was worth it."

"Really?"

"For the ice cream." Her smile was tinged with Oreo crumbs and smears of whipped cream and chocolate sauce. "That's the best Earth invention ever!"

"Hard to argue with that."

"And . . . I think it helped me not be scared anymore. Everyone was so nice and friendly when you came back. I like Earth now." With that she ran over to her classmates, who were taking turns hopping onto Snarffle and riding him down the middle of the road.

When we got back to the B&B, Mrs. Crowzen led the kids upstairs to get them cleaned up, and the adult aliens drifted to their rooms. Amy and I had a chance to talk in the sitting room.

She got right to it. "So why are they here?"

"Still not sure, but I'm meeting them tomorrow morning at the park to figure it out."

"I'm going with you."

I shook my head. "We can't afford to leave the b-and-b without any humans in it. What if the meeting is, like, a diversion or something?"

"Yeah, I guess you're right." She sighed. "It's so weird that they helped us out back there. I wonder what they could possibly want."

"I'll find out tomorrow," I said. "And then we'll have to get rid of them somehow."

"Okay. Tomorrow. But let's try not to worry too much about it tonight." She fell back into an easy chair and exhaled heavily. "Tonight, we should celebrate the fact that we just pulled that off."

"Definitely." I flopped down on the couch and grinned. It felt like the first time in days I'd let my muscles unclench. "Did you see how excited everybody was when they thought they were going to be on TV? We could have buzzed through town on flying polka-dotted elephants and they wouldn't have noticed."

Amy laughed. "Can you imagine my dad trying to do something like that?"

"No way." I sprawled out, put my feet up on the armrest. "You know, as good as Grandma is at all of this stuff, I'm not sure she could have done it, either."

"We really made it happen, didn't we? That girl was lost and we saved her. Just the two of us."

"We did." Her *just the two of us* comment got me thinking. . . . It was quiet. The adult Tourists were all upstairs, and no kid aliens were spying on us. Might it be the time for a little victory kiss?

I made eye contact and started to scooch over in Amy's direction when—

"Wait a minute." She bolted straight up in her chair, worry lines creasing her face. Not exactly the reaction I was going for.

"What? What's the matter?"

"Does this mean that we actually have to make a commercial now?"

Even though I was completely worn out from the day's events, I couldn't sleep at all that night. I kept getting up to double-check the locks on the doors and windows. I guess I never realized how much I had always relied on adults to worry about that kind of stuff.

Finally, about three in the morning, I gave up and went downstairs. I figured I'd make a snack and try to come up with some sort of plan for my big meeting.

As I fumbled my way down the dark hall, I saw a disembodied ghost head floating toward me. I stifled a yell and shrank against the wall, pressing myself into the shadows.

But as it got closer, it turned out to be Cottage Cheese Head wearing a dark robe. He stopped and tilted his lumpy head, giving me a strange look. "Why are you all scrunched up along the wall there?"

"Um...no reason." I stood up straighter, trying to preserve a scrap of dignity. "What are you doing?"

"I was headed to the bathroom, but then I heard something downstairs. Turned out to just be that primitive communication device." He jerked his head in the direction of the stairwell and smiled. "You probably want to check it out."

"All right, thanks. G'night."

I hurried downstairs to the sitting room, and there was Tate, making another guest appearance on the jerry-rigged TV.

His face was drawn and worried, and there were new bags under the eyes. It looked like he had aged ten years.

"I hope everything is okay with you kids and the b-and-b." He was whispering for some reason. "Just keep everything on lockdown until I get back, and you should be fine."

There was a noise off-screen. Tate jerked his head around to glance over his shoulder, then turned toward the screen with a haunted look in his eyes. "My situation here is dire. I've learned some bad news about the ship I'm on. Some very bad news."

Oh, no. It looked like we weren't the only ones with a lot to worry about. For Amy's sake, I hoped he would be all right.

There was another noise behind Tate. Then voices, getting closer.

"They're looking for me." Tate moved closer to the screen, dropped his voice lower. "They won't rest until they find me."

Yikes. What could possibly be hunting him on that—?

"Yoo-hoo!"

"Where are you?"

"You can't stay away forever, you know!" The voices were high-pitched.

Tate twisted his neck to scan the area behind him, then whipped his head back to face me. "Turns out this ship I'm on is...well, it's a...oh, good gravy, I can't even say it. Just too horrible."

One of those shrill voices called out, much louder this time. "You aren't trying to make contact with your home planet again, are you?"

"Because then we know right where you are!"

Tate's words came in a rush. "Turns out this ship is a dang interplanetary singles cruise! And the ladies here are none too particular about staying with their own species. It's my worst nightmare come true."

The door behind him slowly opened.

"Come back to the party, you silly Earth man!"

Tate pressed his face right up to the screen and spoke in a choked whisper. "There are only so many places to hide on this thing." The screen went dark.

Wow.

Well, I wouldn't have believed it could ever happen...but I almost felt sorry for Tate.

22

At least they looked a little better, sitting at the picnic table in blue jeans and T-shirts instead of silvery jumpsuits. And I'm glad they left the body paint at home, especially since there were other people scattered around the park—normal people—throwing Frisbees and skipping rocks across the surface of the Nooksack River.

It didn't take long for me to be reminded, though, that looks can be deceiving.

The man jumped up as I approached and offered me a business card. Across the middle were the letters SPUFOOS. In the lower left-hand corner it said JOE & SUE MAXWELL, along with a Web site address. That's it. Not the best advertising for whatever it was they were selling.

"You can use these names"—he tapped the card, then leaned in and lowered his voice—"but those aren't our real handles, of course. Can't have the government knowing every little thing about us."

The woman—*Sue*, I guess—winked at me. "I'm sure someone in your unique position understands."

Oooookay...

I looked at the card again. "SPUFOOS?" I pronounced it *Spoof Ooze*.

"At your service." The guy took off his baseball cap and actually bowed, and I noticed he was wearing a bad toupee over his bald head. Not quite as hideous as his alien wig, but close.

"I'm sure that our operation has been very useful to you and your people, in your line of work." When the woman smiled at me, her round cheeks bunched up so much they almost made her eyes disappear. "In a way, we're practically in the same business."

"And that's why we've come to see you, to make a little proposition," Joe Maxwell said, settling back down on the bench. "It seems that you have a perfect location for—"

"Wait, what are SPUFOOS?"

They exchanged surprised looks. "Are you joking?"

"No. I've never heard of that."

"SPaceship and UFO Observation Society, of course."

Oh, boy. So that's what we were dealing with here. It all started to make sense—the obsession with aliens, the sneaking around, the mistrust of the government. "Okay, no offense, but are you, like, the kind of people who wear little tinfoil hats to keep the CIA from reading your thought rays or whatever?"

They both burst out laughing.

"You hear that?"

"What a notion!"

"Hats made of tinfoil. Ha!"

The woman shook her head, wiping laugh tears out of her eyes. "*Tinfoil.* You believe that?"

The man looked around the park to make sure that no one was watching, then reached up and peeled off that horrible toupee. He flipped it over and pointed to the metallic lining that covered the entire inside of the wig. Leaning forward and using that conspiratorial tone again, he said, "It's all titanium these days. We found out a long time ago that mere tinfoil lets out over fifty percent of the thought rays." He fixed the toupee back on his head. "I wear my protection at all times."

"Ri-i-ight. Good thinking." Yikes. I never imagined that their human outfits would be even freakier than their alien costumes.

"And it's not actually the CIA, of course," Sue chimed in. "The government organizations with the real power don't exactly advertise their existence to the general public." She winked again. "But then you know all about keeping things secret from the public, don't you?"

"Not really." I started to back away. "Look, this is all some kind of big misunderstanding. We don't actually—"

They both jumped out of their seats.

"Wait!"

"Don't go!"

"Hear us out. We owe you an apology."

I did not want these two showing up at the B&B again. Maybe if I stayed and heard them out, they would just leave. "I promised ten minutes. You have eight left."

"Okay." The man cleared his throat. "We realize now that we should not have stopped by unannounced."

"Or in costume," Sue said.

"Or uninvited," I added. "Or at all."

"But we wanted to check out your place for ourselves," Joe hurried on, "and thought we'd have to do it surreptitious-like. From the inside. Trust me—we understand that you have a vested interest in keeping your operation a secret from the general public."

"Not really." I tried to keep my expression and voice as neutral as possible. It was crucial to maintain a good poker face. "We're running a bed-and-breakfast. It wouldn't exactly be good for business to keep that a secret from potential customers."

Sue gave me a knowing smile. "Not your *real* customers, anyway."

I did not like where this was going at all. "What's that supposed to mean?"

"Let's just put all our cards on the table," Joe said, spreading his arms wide. "We happen to know that you are harboring genuine space aliens at your establishment."

And there it was.

I had no choice but to forge ahead with the big bluff. "Seriously? Just because we have an outer-space theme and do alien-costume events, like the commercial yesterday?" I forced out a fake chuckle. "What, do you think that *Star Wars* is a documentary? Or maybe that *The Hitchhiker's Guide to the Galaxy* is a real travel handbook?"

Sue reached out and patted me on the arm. "You don't have to hide anything from us. We told you already, we're on your side."

Joe Maxwell nodded. "And trust us, we don't want the government finding out about your operation any more than you do."

Sue *tsk-tsked.* "They would muck everything up something awful. Just look at the mess they made down at Area Fifty-one in Roswell. Why, that could've been the most miraculous discovery of the last century, and they go and—"

"Again, no offense, but do you two believe in *everything?* Goblins and werewolves and vampires? All of it?"

"Of course not!" They both scoffed and made disgusted faces.

Sue sniffed. "We are perfectly capable of distinguishing between fantasy and reality."

"That's right," Joe Maxwell said. "Ghosts and monsters and all the rest—those are the inventions of people, meant to frighten or amuse. Pure fiction. We have no interest in such things."

"Plus, they're just downright icky." Sue shuddered. "We don't want anything to do with those kinds of scary stories."

"But aliens," Joe Maxwell said, "are a different matter entirely. Life on other planets is a mathematical inevitability. Why, the Kepler telescope has already found hundreds of Earth-like planets, and that project is just getting started."

"And think about it," Sue said. "There are over two

thousand billion *billion* suns in the known universe. So if you think there's only a one-in-a-billion chance that another planet could sustain life, then that still means there are billions of planets with aliens on them out there!"

"And if you take into consideration—"

"I get it." I held up my hands for silence. I had heard all of this stuff before, from Amy. "Let's say I totally agree with you, okay? There is a one hundred percent chance of alien life out there. Granted. But now it's your turn to trust me." They leaned forward, eyes wide, eager for the big reveal. "There's a zero percent chance that any of those aliens are sleeping at the Intergalactic Bed and Breakfast."

They sighed and their faces fell. "We're very disappointed to hear you say that, young man."

"Not nearly as disappointed as I am to have to get up early and come all the way down here to say it." I turned and started walking away. "Enjoy the rest of your time in Forest Grove."

"You really don't want to leave," Sue said.

I waved good-bye without turning around.

"I hope you have room at the b-and-b for around ten thousand people or so," Joe Maxwell called.

I stopped. This time I did turn around. "Why do you say that?"

Joe lifted his palms in a gesture that looked almost apologetic. "Because that's about how many people we can summon to town this weekend to have a look at your place."

Sue winked yet again. "For starters."

23

I couldn't afford to just leave and pray that it was only a bluff.

"Do you mind telling me why you're so convinced that E.T. is a regular customer of ours?" I walked back to the picnic table.

Sue's cheeks bunched up as she beamed at me again. "That's more like it." She reached under the bench and used two hands to hoist up a big photo album, crammed to bursting with papers and photos. Then she cheerfully patted the seat next to her. "We really don't want to do this the hard way, you know. We'd much rather have you on board with us."

I sighed and slumped down on the bench. As Sue flipped through the pages of the album, I caught glimpses of the contents—tabloid sketches of big-eyed, long-necked gray aliens, a flyer announcing the Annual SPUFOOS Mountaintop Lookout Party—until Sue got to the middle and slowed down.

"Ah, yes, here we are."

She stopped on a clipping of the front page of the *Forest Grove Gazette* (complete with a picture of some aliens I had taken on a camping trip last summer and then kinda, you know, lost control of). The next was a *Newsweek* article about the time when the nearby Nooksack River had frozen solid in an instant (okay, something else I had done—completely by accident, I promise—with the doomsday device belonging to an alien criminal mastermind). The next was from the *Gazette* again, this article detailing the mysterious depressions in the brick courtyard of the town commons that had appeared overnight without explanation (from when a huge ship of alien slave traders landed there because I had failed to convince everyone that our transporter repairman was an evil genius).

It was like a Greatest Hits collection of all my worst mistakes.

Joe Maxwell tapped the photo album. "We've had our eye on this place for several years now."

Sue nodded. "There were always little red flags popping up, for those who know how and where to look."

"And we're always looking, aren't we, sweetie?"

The two shared an affectionate glance. "It's been our life's work." When they reached out to hold hands—I swear I'm not making this up—their fingers were in the shape of the *Star Trek* "Live Long and Prosper" sign.

Kooks in love. Very heartwarming.

Joe Maxwell gestured to the photo album with his free hand. "But it wasn't until last summer that the suspicious activity really started ratcheting up."

Right when I started working for Grandma. What a coincidence.

"And when the most unusual things started happening this summer, we knew that we had finally found what we'd been looking for all these years." Sue sighed happily. "It was time for a long-overdue trip to Forest Grove."

"And you certainly haven't disappointed us." Joe continued to flip through the album, displaying newly pasted aerial shots of the alien kids playing in Grandma's backyard. Those must have been taken from that hot air balloon.

But there were other things in there, too. Like a Forest Grove Fourth of July fireworks-show flyer with rough sketches of Frog Face and some other aliens. Sue and Joe must have made that after Amy and I took away their camera. And one of our fake posters advertising an upcoming alien masquerade ball.

As I saw how intently they were gazing at that stuff, I realized that maybe it could also give me a way out. "Look, is that what you want? Things connected to the b-and-b? For you and all of the friends you claim are going to be showing up?"

"Spoofies," Joe said.

"What?"

"The loyal followers of SPUFOOS. We call them *Spoofies*."

"Of course you do." It was hard to keep a straight face.

How much weirder were these two going to get? "So would you like some souvenirs for them?"

Sue sniffed and put her arms over the album protectively. "These are important historical documents, not *souvenirs*."

"Whatever. But is that what you want? Stuff? Because I can get you some stuff." The Tourists were always leaving little things behind. Spare change that came in the form of glowing cubes, or pieces of strange jewelry, or whatever. Harmless stuff. And it's not like anyone would believe any *Spoofies* if they claimed to be in possession of genuine alien artifacts.

If that's what got them all excited—and if it meant they would just go away—I'd gladly hand over a sack full of that junk.

Joe Maxwell shook his head sadly. "I'm afraid we're not interested in trinkets, young man."

I sighed. "Then what are you interested in?"

They exchanged a meaningful glance, then looked at me again. "Okay. Here it is." Joe Maxwell took a deep breath. "We'd like to set up SPUFOOS headquarters at the Intergalactic Bed and Breakfast."

My facial expression must have perfectly matched what I was thinking, because they rushed on before I could say no.

"Let us explain! It would be the perfect setup."

"For everyone involved."

"It would be the ideal marriage of form and function."

I made a *wrap-it-up* gesture. "Two minutes left."

"It has been our life's mission to document alien visitations to Earth." Joe Maxwell slipped off the bench and hunkered down in front of me, practically begging on his knees. "What better place to do that than at a vacation hot spot for extraterrestrial travelers?"

"We've had to make do with mostly unreliable eyewitness accounts from all over the world." Sue put her hands on her husband's shoulders and leaned over him eagerly—they almost looked like a two-headed alien sharing the same body. They were certainly sharing the same crazy notions. "Being able to base our operations from the Grand Central Station of off-world depots would be the culmination of all our hopes and dreams."

"We could finally become humanity's ambassadors to the rest of the universe." Their eyes were filled with such longing that I almost felt bad for them.

But not really.

"Sorry. Time's up."

They didn't jump up this time or come toward me as I backed away. They just looked at me sadly.

"We really don't want to do this the hard way," Joe Maxwell said.

"It's not our style." Sue sighed. "But we will if we have to."

I stopped backing up. "Look, you seem like nice people. I didn't want to have to come right out and say this, but one of our employees was sheriff in this town for over twenty years. He can have a restraining order filed against you just like that." I snapped my fingers. "And then if you—or any of your friends—get within a hundred yards of the b-and-b, I'm afraid you'll be arrested."

They shared another meaningful look. "Oh, yes? And just where is this officer of the law?" Joe Maxwell said.

Uh-oh. Not a good question.

"We haven't seen him around here in a few days. It's almost as if he's disappeared into thin air."

"Or into the atmosphere, you might say."

"You know"—Sue cupped her chin in her hand, making a show of mulling something over—"he's been missing almost as long as the proprietor of the business, hasn't he?"

Joe Maxwell gave an exaggerated nod. "Now that you mention it, I haven't seen either one of them in days. In fact, it almost seems like the entire operation is being run by a couple of kids."

"Hmmmmm." When Sue smiled this time, her expression looked more hungry than happy. "That's certainly good timing for us, isn't it?"

I swallowed. And stood there. What could I say?

They let me stew in the uncomfortable silence for a few moments before Joe said, "Well, what about it? Care to give us a little tour of the bed and breakfast?"

"Give me some time to think about it," I blurted out. Stalling: the last resort when you don't have a plan. Maybe Amy would be able to help me figure something out.

Joe and Sue looked at each other, then back at me. "We've been waiting our entire lives, so I guess we could give it the rest of the day." Sue checked her watch. "We'll meet you right back here at nine o'clock this evening."

Joe cleared his throat. "But after that, I'm afraid we'll be getting into that house, one way or another."

"With all of our friends," Sue added.

24

I raced to the library before heading back to the B&B. Although Grandma's house was the only place on Earth with interstellar transporters, it still didn't have Internet access. I wanted a look at that Web site before I talked to Amy.

It was worse than I thought.

The home page was no-frills, just an outer space background with links to UFO-related updates and events. But it was easy to tell that people regularly visited the site. A lot of people.

On the UFO Reports page, I could see at a glance that several sightings were posted every day, and hundreds of official reports were filed every month. And not only from every state in the union, but also just about every country in the world. India, South Korea, New Zealand, even someplace called Azerbaijan.

Some of the descriptions were really specific. *Three rotating, multicolored lights floating just above the horizon for 45 minutes, moving in a southeasterly direction.* Others were not. *A big fireball shot right over campus!* But every day, tons of people were making reports.

And these were people who liked to travel and congregate. A glance at the post titles revealed that this month alone you could visit the UFO International Congress in Nevada, the Mutual UFO Network Symposium in Colorado, the Little Green Man Festival in Kentucky, or the UFO Festival in Oregon.

And just how many people might travel all the way to little Forest Grove?

Unfortunately, it wasn't hard to find the answer.

I clicked on the *Breaking News!* banner:

Biggest Discovery Ever?

Dear Friends, Followers, and Fellow Believers:

As you know if you visit this site regularly, we do our best to weed out the hoaxes and the pranksters to bring you the most valid and up-to-date official reports of UFO sightings. It is not now—nor has it ever been —our practice to indulge in idle speculation or baseless gossip. So we hope that our decades of work on maintaining this site will lend credibility and weight to this amazing announcement. We have very good reason to believe that we have found the mother lode. The UFO seekers' promised land. The alien lovers' nirvana. Whatever you want to call it, this will make Roswell look like a minor historical footnote. Currently, our investigation is under way, but if things turn out as we think they will, we will soon be ready to announce a location where aliens have been visiting Earth on a regular basis for several years.

Yes, you read that right.

Please check back with this site often. Once the official announcement is made, we would like people to join us in visiting this amazing place. We think it would be the perfect new setting for SPUFOOS head-quarters, and we may need your help in making this happen.

Stay tuned. Until then, keep watching the sky!

—Joe and Sue Maxwell

But the article wasn't even the worst part. That honor went to the comments section:

Keep up the great work. You know we'll be there!
—Spoofies-for-life Bill and Wilma Hoople,
Astoria, Oregon

The RV's all packed up and ready to go. Just give us the coordinates.
—Randy and Megan Anderson,
Duluth, Minnesota

At your service, as always.
　　　　　　　　　—The UFO Society of Burley, Idaho

Finally! Can't wait to visit the site with you! (And congratulations!!!!!)
　　　　　　—Your humble servants Doug and Lisa Byrnes,
　　　　　　　　Riverside, Iowa (Proud Future Birthplace
　　　　　　　　　　of Captain James Tiberius Kirk)

The comments went on and on. I didn't read them all, but a quick scan confirmed that everyone seemed pretty eager to visit this amazing new place.

I did not doubt that Joe and Sue Maxwell, as loopy as they were, could bring a whole heck of a lot of people to the front door of the Intergalactic Bed & Breakfast. I printed out the article and a few pages of comments, then ran back to Grandma's place to talk to Amy. We had to come up with a plan. Fast.

25

Amy was waiting for me on the front porch. "How'd it go?"

"Not good." I panted, trying to get my breathing under control. "They run this operation called SPUFOOS. It stands for the—"

"SPaceship and UFO Observation Society."

I blinked a few times. "You've heard of them?"

Amy put her hands on her hips and gave me that look that girls give you when they think you've said something really stupid, only you have no idea why they're looking at you like that or what you might have said wrong or how you could have possibly said it any differently. That look went on for kind of a long time.

"Sooooo...I guess that's a yes, then? You *have* heard of them."

Amy blew her bangs out of her face. "David, a UFO reporting center is the very first thing that we talked about when we met last summer."

Oh...

The look she was giving me turned into more of a glare. "Don't boys remember anything important?"

Important? Sure, it was important *now*, because the kooks had shown up with their costumes and their threats, but how was I supposed to know it was so important *then*? Amy had talked about a lot of weird things when I first met her.

"Give me a break. I remember everything else about that day," I said.

"Okay." She crossed her arms over her chest. "What was I wearing?"

Seriously??? "Ummm...clothes?"

Amy sighed. "Like I said, boys don't remember anything."

"Oh, yeah? Okay, what was *I* wearing, then?"

She scoffed. "That's easy. Same shirt you're wearing right now."

"I already told you, it's okay to wear the same thing a lot in the summer! The, um, the fashion rules are different when you're on vacation."

"Whatever." She sighed again. "You probably haven't even washed it since then."

I took a deep breath. "Look, Grandma and your dad have left the planet, we just took a group of undisguised aliens into town, and there are UFO-crazy kooks stalking the place and making threats. Do you really want to talk about my shirt?"

"You shouldn't call them *kooks*."

"It's better than *Spoofies!*"

"It's not like they're crazy or anything, David."

"Oh, really? Maybe you missed the silver jumpsuits and the full body paint and the wigs?"

Amy had a hurt expression. "Not everyone who's interested in outer space is a kooky loser, you know."

Girls. You think you're talking about one thing with them, but you've really been talking about something else all along.

"I didn't mean someone like *you*, obviously. You have a job working with actual aliens. You know that all of this stuff is real. They're just guessing."

"Pretty good guessing, then. Let's see, they think that aliens are visiting Earth, and they've tracked them here to the b-and-b. Just a lucky guess, though, right?"

I had no idea what to say. Thankfully, a clatter of laughter drifted through the open window, serving as a welcome distraction.

"What's that?"

Amy shrugged. "It's just the kids. I think they're watching something on TV."

We listened to the young aliens buzz and honk and squeal for a few moments. I was hoping that it would kind of break the tension.

"Okay." Time to try again. "I get it. These SPUFOOS folks—however they pulled it off—have stumbled across something real. But that's what I'm afraid of. That's what makes them so dangerous."

I filled Amy in on the entire conversation, then showed her the pages I had printed out from the Web site. "I don't doubt that they could get thousands of people here on short notice."

"Neither do I. Their operation is very well known in the UFO-watchdog community. And it's true, they do their best to weed out pranks and hoaxes, so they have sort of legitimized UFO reporting." She tapped the SPUFOOS logo on the sheet of paper. "I told you last summer—not that you remember—that the headquarters are here in Washington State."

"Yikes. That probably made it easier for them to monitor this place, huh?"

"Oh, I'm sure. Rumor has it that the Maxwells invested in Microsoft when it was just a start-up, and retired early. Now they have the money and the time to monitor the sighting reports pretty much around the clock." Amy exhaled heavily. "If anyone ever had a chance of figuring out our big secret, I suppose it had to be them."

"I guess the answer is simple, then. We have to convince them that they're wrong."

Amy ran her hands through her hair. "And just how are we going to do that? By nine o'clock tonight?"

"I have absolutely no idea."

We were interrupted by another burst of alien laughter. Kanduu stuck his little head out the window. "Come quickly! You two have to witness this." So we went back inside, where we found all of the kid aliens huddled around the TV.

They were watching another amazing episode of *The Tate Show*.

It took me a little while to figure out it was him, though. Amy's horrified gasp was a tip-off. He was wearing this full-body, one-piece outfit. The material was black and sleek and shiny—like something you'd see on an action star in a futuristic movie—but it was also skintight, so it just made him look even more bulbous.

Even worse, the outfit was sprouting all of these long, leathery growths that looked like oversize porcupine quills. To top it off, there was this black headdress thing fanning out from the back of the neck area and over his head like a display of burnt peacock tail feathers.

It was quite the fashion statement.

But instead of strutting on an alien catwalk, Tate was lumbering around the room as fast as he could, those porcupine quills bouncing all over. He grabbed furniture, hoisted it in the air, and then crashed it back to the ground in three piles around the room.

At first I thought he looked like an alien, but that wasn't it, exactly. More like some kind of crazed monster.

"What is he *doing?*"

"Trying to make a barricade in front of all the entrance points," Kanduu said.

"But it doesn't work!" One of the former slime-drippers said. "Watch this—it's my favorite part."

Tate was struggling to stack a bunch of shiny chrome chairs in front of one of the doors. But the chairs were all so varied and oddly shaped—to fit the contours of many different types of alien bodies—that they kept falling down around him. One crashed onto his foot, and Tate let loose a string of colorful curses.

"What do those human words mean?" Kandeel squeaked. "My translator's not picking them up."

"Never mind," Amy said. She was bent over in a full-body

cringe, watching the TV through cracks between the fingers that were hiding her face. "Oh, poor Dad."

As soon as Tate managed to construct a shaky-but-standing tower of chairs, the door on the other side of the room was forced open an inch or two, thumping into another furniture blockade. When Tate raced over to fortify that barrier, the tower behind him fell apart, scattering chairs all over the room.

Lots more cursing. And this time even I didn't recognize all of the words.

The alien kids howled with laughter, pointing at the screen and making a running commentary on the action.

When the barricades were as stable as they were going to get, Tate approached the screen. The tight outfit made his walking motion sort of a lurch, and he looked like some kind of bloated spider/porcupine/bird-of-prey hybrid monster. The only halfway recognizable part of him was the round face sticking out of that shiny black material.

The fact that I was not laughing hysterically was proof of how much I liked Amy.

"Kids." Tate's voice was an urgent, husky whisper. "You wouldn't believe the things I've had to endure. I mean, just *look* at this ridiculous outfit! They forced it on me and claimed they had to take my uniform and wash it to get rid of the alien germs and microbes and whatnot. Can you believe that? They called *me* an alien!"

One of the doors thumped against a furniture tower again, sending a few more chrome chairs tumbling to the floor. A thin green arm covered in exotic jewelry snaked through the crack in the doorway and pushed more furniture out of the way.

"You can't stay cooped up in there forever, you know!" called a shrill voice. "The party's still going and everyone wants to see you dancing again!"

Dancing?

Tate??

Again???

Tate shook his head furiously at the screen, feathers flying everywhere as his ridiculous headdress swayed back and forth. "That wasn't dancing, I swear," he whispered. "I was just trying to run away!"

I glanced at Amy. She couldn't even look at the TV anymore.

Onscreen, an overstuffed love seat scraped along the floor as a second door was forced partway open. "The slow dances are about to start. Come out of your hidey-hole, you adorable little Earth creature!"

Yikes. That must be one ginormous lady alien if she was calling Tate "little."

"Listen! I don't have much time." Tate spat out a few dark feathers and pushed his face right up to the screen. "If your grandmother beats me home, tell her she's got to try to help me get out of here. She can use her contacts with the Hoteliers Association, or call in a favor with an old customer. Anything." Tate whipped his head around as the furniture towers teetered on the edge of collapse. All of the doors were opening inch by inch.

Tate's desperate eyes shot back to the screen. "Tell her I'll do anything to pay her back. *Anything.* Just hurry!"

Then the screen went black. The kid aliens fell over each other in a heap, bodies convulsing with laughter. "Again!" They all shouted. "Show it again!"

The screen flickered back to life and here came the replay of Tate running around the room. Amy moved to turn the TV off when—

Ding!

The sound that signified the arrival of more Tourists.

I looked at Amy. "I thought you shut down the transporters."

Ding!

"I did," she said. "But I had to leave at least one on for when Dad and your grandma finally come back, remember?" She glanced at the TV and swallowed. "*If* they come back."

"Which transporter did you leave on?"

"The one in the cellar. Hardly any Tourists ever come in that way. I figured we'd be safe."

Ding! Ding!

Perfect. Just what the situation needed.

More aliens.

The family of space Tourists that emerged from the cellar was definitely not of the disguisable variety.

Sure, all of their features were more or less humanoid, covered with skin instead of scales, and they each had the recommended number of earthling body parts. But it still wasn't going to work.

The first one I saw had the impossibly long tree-trunk legs of an NBA center, yet a really small torso, with arms and head balanced up top. It looked like a toddler on six-foot stilts.

The rest of them were similarly mismatched in terms

of proportion. Overly long orangutan arms on a body with stubby little munchkin legs. An adult-size head sitting on top of a kindergarten-size alien. It looked like the entire family had been thrown into a blender on the highest setting.

They smiled and waved, but I couldn't muster up much of a welcoming response. "Hi, folks. Thanks for coming, but I'm afraid you're not going to be able to stay here. There's no way we can disguise you enough for an Earth vacation." I tried not to sound too rude, but we really didn't have time for this.

Amy stepped forward. "I'm so sorry," she said. "We can offer a full refund. You've caught us at a bad time."

There was never going to be a good time for these par-ticular Tourists to come here—didn't anybody read the *Your Vacation on Earth!* brochure anymore?—but I didn't say that. I just wanted them gone as quickly as possible.

One of them stepped forward. "What is the problem?" The face and voice suggested that this one might be the dad, but he was also the one with the tiniest body. It would have been funny under less frantic circumstances.

"We just don't have any disguises that would fit you," Amy said. "Earthlings are shaped more like..." She waved her arms around and stuck one leg out on display. "Like this, I guess."

The kindergarten-size dad smiled. "Oh, that shouldn't be a problem."

"What?" I was getting annoyed—this was a total waste of time. "There is no way the clothes we have are going to fit you, and even if they did, we couldn't—"

"Okay, gang, let's get into formation for this planet." Tiny

Dad turned to face his family, completely ignoring me. "Use these two as a guide." He jerked his oversize head toward Amy and me.

The alien with the too-long arms tilted his head to study me for a moment, then reached up to grab at his shoulder. He got a firm grip . . . and pulled his arm right out of the socket. It made sort of a wet squelching sound.

But there was no blood. No screaming in pain. He just popped it right off his body. The long arm rested on the floor as it dangled from his grip, the fingers still flexing and grasping in an extremely creepy fashion.

The suddenly one-armed alien looked around the room, then called out to one of his taller siblings. "Hey, here you go. This'll look better on you for this planet." He got a grip on the elbow and tossed the whole thing with a sidearm delivery, like a Frisbee. It sailed across the room and smacked his sister in the stomach.

"Ouch! Don't throw it so hard." She popped off one of her own stubby arms and replaced it with the new one. It looked much better on her long torso, more normally proportioned. Normal for an earthling look, anyway.

The rest of the aliens sized up Amy and me for a minute, and then they all began to pull off arms and legs. Soon the floor was piled high with wriggling, writhing limbs.

They all walked or crawled or slithered around the room (depending on how many appendages they had left), inspecting the body parts.

Then everyone put themselves back together in a blur of activity. They had obviously done this before.

One little girl alien walked up to Amy, staring at her face.

"Oooohhh...those facial markings are so cute. Can I try them on?" She reached up and tried to pluck a few of Amy's freckles right off her nose.

"Ouch." Amy backed up. "I'm sorry—I'd, um, like to share, but I'm afraid these are stuck on pretty good."

"Oh." The girl studied Amy's face. "Really? That's weird." She went back to trading body parts with her siblings. Soon the family stood in the middle of the room and put their new looks on display, waggling their arms and legs around like they were doing the Hokey Pokey. "How do we look?" the mom said when they were all done.

We just stared at them. They had quickly transformed into something that could actually pass for a human family.

Amy found her voice first. "Yeah. You look great, actually."

"Dad!" one of the younger aliens called. "Here's an extra." He stepped forward holding an arm that was flopping around in his grip.

"Whoops!" the dad said. (He looked much better at six feet tall than he had at two and a half.) "It's like a jigsaw puzzle, isn't it? Always find one piece missing just when you think you're done." He turned to his family and waved the little arm around as the fingers clawed the air grotesquely. "Who needs this?"

Behind us, our kid aliens, who were still watching Tate, erupted into another burst of laughter. I turned to see Tate's face grow red on the screen as he lumbered around, but I couldn't find the humor in it anymore. Instead, all I could think about was how much madder Tate would be if he came back and there were ten thousand UFO seekers surrounding the house.

If I thought he looked like a scary monster now, I certainly didn't want to be around when he—

"Wait a minute."

Amy looked at me and frowned. "Who are you talking to?"

"Myself." I waved her off, deep in thought. I looked back and forth from Monster Tate to the Switching Body Parts family. A little boy had emerged from the back of the pack to grab the little arm and affix it to his body. It was creepy, but for what I suddenly had in mind it was creepy in a very good way.

"I think I have a plan." I really did. I nodded. It could work. "I've got it!"

"Got what?" Amy said.

"Sir," I addressed the dad. "That thing you all do with your arms and legs…" I waved vaguely at them. "Could you, um …Do you think you could do that with your heads?"

The dad smiled. And then he reached up with both hands and pulled his head right off his neck with the sound of wet Velcro. Cradling his head casually in the crook of one arm, he said, "You mean like this?" His smile looked pretty gruesome, seeing as how it was now a foot below his shoulders.

I turned to Amy. Her face had gone white and was all twisted with disgust, like maybe she wanted to throw up.

That was fantastic.

"I finally have it," I said.

"What are you talking about?"

"A way to convince those UFO watchers that they don't want any part of this house."

I paced around, my mind whirling, as everyone watched me. Finally I turned back to Amy. "Can you run to the store for me?"

"Why?"

"Ketchup," I said.

"*What?*"

"Ketchup. We're going to need a lot of it." I ran to the drawer where Grandma kept the petty cash and pulled out a wad of bills, which I thrust at Amy. "Buy as many bottles as you can carry, then meet me back here."

I'd had small roles in a few plays when I was in elementary school, so I knew a little bit about what it took to get ready. Props. Set design. Decorations. Costumes.

But back then we had six weeks to prepare, sometimes longer. Opening night for our production at the B&B would take place in less than twelve hours.

At least I had an enthusiastic crew. I was a little nervous about how my plan would go over with all of the Tourists, but they took to it right away. It would give them something to do, and besides, I think they thought it was kind of funny.

I was hoping that Joe and Sue Maxwell, UFO Watchdogs Extraordinaire, would feel otherwise.

I handed out jobs and everyone got to work. Grandma had a ton of supplies in her storage sheds and in the basement, but we still had to make a few store runs. I sent Amy on those—I didn't want any aliens leaving the house, and I needed to be around to supervise the work party.

By the time I had to go meet with the Maxwells, everything was in place. Well, kind of. The dress rehearsal wasn't perfect, that's for sure, but I was hoping that performing in the near dark would mask some of the sloppiness of the rush job on production.

Amy and I were out on the porch at quarter to nine as I got ready for my second meeting down at the park. Studying myself in the window's reflection, I messed up my hair, then tucked in half of my shirt and left the other half hanging out.

"What kind of a look are you going for there?" Amy said.

I untied one of my shoes. "Disheveled."

Amy regarded me with one raised eyebrow. "Mission accomplished."

I kept looking at my reflection and practiced making desperately-worried-and-horrified facial expressions. "My performance starts before the one back here, remember?"

Amy moved closer and put her hand on my arm. Her voice was quiet. "David. Do you think this is going to work?"

"I have no idea."

She flashed me her lopsided smile. That freckle patch on her nose crinkled up. So cute. Man, I must really like her if I noticed something like that at a time like this. But my stomach was still all twisted up with nerves.

"What are you smiling about?" I said.

"That's just one of the things I like about you."

"What do you mean?"

"Trying something is always better than doing nothing. Most people do nothing. All the time." She reached up and mussed my hair a little more. "But you try stuff even if you don't know that it's going to work. Even if it has, in fact, very little chance of working."

Was she making fun of me? "Um, thanks...I think." I checked the time. Again. "I guess I better get going."

Amy leaned over and gave me a quick peck on the cheek. "You'll do great."

Now it was my turn to smile. And I even felt better as I made my way through the gate and down the road. Like maybe I could do almost anything, after all.

· 🪐 ·

I ran most of the way to the park, not because I was a little late (that was planned—it would be better for them to be there waiting for me), but because I wanted to be out of breath.

The sky was getting dusky by the time I made it to the park, but I could see Joe and Sue over at the same picnic table. I turned the speed up a notch and raced across the softball fields. As soon as I knew they were watching me, I craned my neck and glanced over my shoulder, in the direction of the B&B, then whipped my head back again. I did this a few times.

When I got to the table I collapsed onto the opposite bench, panting heavily. I stared over their shoulders, into the distance, focusing on nothing.

"Oh, my. Are you okay, young man?"

"Whatever is the matter?"

The look of genuine concern on their faces made me feel a little bit bad. After all, they did seem like nice people. But then I thought about ten thousand nice people invading Forest Grove. That made it easier to continue.

"It's started again...." I tried to make my voice shaky, but I didn't want to overdo it. It came out in sort of a choppy whisper.

Joe Maxwell stood up. "What's started?"

"Is everything all right?" Sue got up and started to come around to my side of the table, but I waved her off.

"It's happening. Again." I searched the darkening sky. "Oh, no..."

"What?"

"There's going to be a full moon tonight, isn't there? It's always the worst when there's a full moon." I figured someone who watched the sky as much as they did must be aware of the phases of the moon.

Joe Maxwell nodded, his forehead lined with confusion. "As a matter of fact, there is. But what does that have to do with the bed-and—"

"Not here!" I hunched my shoulders and scanned the park, making it look like I was searching for eavesdroppers. There were none, of course, but I lowered my voice anyway. "I can't tell you here. If anyone finds out, the b-and-b will be ruined. You have to come see for yourself."

They exchanged a meaningful glance. "See what?" Sue said, her voice a little breathy with excitement.

I took a deep breath, then let it out slow. They leaned over the picnic table eagerly. I took in another big breath. More leaning until they were practically lying on top of the table.

I lowered my eyes and winced, as if giving up the secret was actually painful.

"You were right."

"We were?" They looked at each other again.

I nodded slowly. "Yes. About the bed-and-breakfast. There's something...something very, very strange going on there. Something secret. Unnatural. Not of this world."

"I knew it!" Joe said. He sprang up and waved his arms in the air in triumph, then swept Sue up in a bear hug, lifting her right off the picnic bench.

Sue grabbed Joe's head with both hands, knocking his toupee sideways. "We found it! We finally found it!" She was basically screaming right in his face.

He certainly didn't mind. He laughed and swung her around some more. "How many years have we been at it? And now we finally get to see..."

Joe trailed off. He must have finally looked over and noticed me. I had dropped my head into my hands and was shaking it back and forth.

"Young man? What's the matter?"

"We already told you, dear, we're on your side."

I brought my head up carefully, as if it weighed a hundred pounds.

Then I slowly dropped my hands from my face. And were there a few tears there, shining in my eyes, as I bravely held them in? I think there were. Man, I was a better actor than I thought. "It's true—there is something strange going on in that house." I shuddered all over for effect. "But it's not aliens."

Their faces crumpled. "What do you mean?"

"Nothing. Look, I've already said too much." I pushed myself away from the table and stood up. "You know, I really shouldn't be dragging you into this. You seem like nice people. Just take my advice and stay far away from that place."

"Oh, no." Sue frowned and wagged her finger at me. "You're not getting rid of us that easily."

"Please. I promise, this is not something you want to see. Not something you want to get mixed up in."

I took a few backward steps, but the Maxwells came out from behind the picnic table and hurried toward me. Joe bent over and looked me in the eyes. "Young man, we have been waiting our entire lives to get into a house like that."

Sue stepped up next to him until all three of us were crammed into my personal-space bubble. "And we'll be getting in there with or without your blessing."

I sighed heavily. I glanced over my shoulder in the direction of the house, then at the ground. "Okay," I mumbled. "Meet me around the back of the b-and-b. At midnight."

"Midnight?"

"Why does it matter when—"

"Trust me." I turned around and started walking away. After a few steps I stopped and twisted around to face them. "But never say that I didn't warn you."

29

At five minutes to midnight, Amy and I were wrapped up in our sleeping bags on the back porch. The full moon gave the surrounding forest a silver sheen.

We didn't talk much. The house was as prepared as it was going to get—everyone inside hopefully ready and waiting in their places—and this thing was either going to work or it wasn't. Instead we just watched the stars until we finally heard muffled whispers and scraping noises moving along the side of the house.

"Showtime."

Amy nodded and gave me a thumbs-up.

Joe and Sue Maxwell appeared at the foot of the stairs, blinking up at us in the moonlight.

"What are you kids doing out here?"

I put my finger over my lips and cast a worried look at the house. Then I crawled out of the sleeping bag and made my way down the steps, followed by Amy.

"We never sleep inside on full moon nights," I whispered.

"Never." Amy also cast an uneasy glance at the house and quickly looked away.

"This is Amy," I said. "She works here too. And she is aware of . . . you know, everything we talked about."

Joe and Sue Maxwell nodded, but they were obviously distracted. "Are you going to let us in the house now?" Joe leaned forward eagerly.

Amy gasped. "Are you really sure you want to do that?" She looked at me, wide-eyed. "I thought you were going to talk them out of it."

"Believe me, I tried. They're very determined."

"Indeed we are." Sue's tight little smile did not make its way to her eyes. "Now if you don't mind, let's drop the cloak-and-dagger routine and get started with the tour, shall we?"

I shot Amy another exaggeratedly worried glance and then sighed as I looked back at Joe and Sue. "If you insist." I lifted a camping lantern off the porch steps and walked along the back of the house. "Follow me."

We made our way to the set of storm doors that led down into the underground cellar. Joe helped me force them open, and the rusty hinges protested with a screech. It was a nice touch.

Only the top few stairs were visible; the rest plunged into the blackness below. I stepped down and turned on the lantern. The sphere of light it cast made it possible for us to slowly make our way down, but it was still plenty gloomy.

We stopped at the base of the stairs, the lantern creating a parade of shadows from all of the clutter and oddly angled walls that formed a maze of hallways. It was like a rabbit warren down there.

"Before we go any farther, I need to tell you the whole truth," I said.

Sue was brushing cobwebs out of her hair. Perfect. "Yes? And what is that?"

"Well, about the house . . . I already told you, we don't have aliens here. But something way worse is going on. Something that explains all of the bizarre things that happen around here. And why we have to be so secretive." I took a deep breath. "The house is . . . well, you see, for as long as anyone can remember, the house has been . . ."

"Go on, David. Just say it," Amy whispered.

"This house is haunted."

I was expecting a bigger reaction, but Joe and Sue Maxwell just looked confused for a few moments, then they both shook their heads and scoffed loudly. "Oh, we already told you, we don't believe in that nonsense." Joe said. "Pure fiction."

Sue pursed her lips and gave a dismissive wave. "And we have no interest in it, either. That stuff is icky."

"We also told you that we aren't going to be easy to get

rid of. This is very disappointing." Joe leaned forward and squinted at what could be seen of the murky cellar. "If you're not going to give us a proper tour, I suppose we'll just have to summon all of our friends and do this the hard way."

"And we'll come in through the *front* door. At a decent hour of the day." Sue sniffed and turned to go back up the stairs.

Amy gasped again, right on cue.

"What is it?" I said.

"L-l-l-look," she breathed.

Joe Maxwell just shook his head and moved to join his wife on the stairs. "If you honestly think we're going to be afraid of a dark basement and some—"

"*Shhhhhh!*"

Joe fell silent. Amy hid behind me, clinging to my arm and peering around my shoulder into the darkened reaches of the cellar.

"What was that?" she said.

"I don't know."

I held up the lantern as we shuffled forward together.

"Not sure I want to know...."

"There!" Amy pointed to a rustling movement up ahead, but it could have just been a shifting shadow as the lantern swayed a little in my grip.

We pretended to ignore Joe and Sue Maxwell and crept deeper into the cellar. Amy squeezed my shoulder when we heard their feet scraping along the cement floor, following us.

Amy let out a little shriek and we both froze. The Maxwells stumbled to a stop just behind us. The movement up ahead was now unmistakably distinct from the surrounding shadows.

I held the lantern over my head and out as far in front of me as I could, casting a dim circle of light ahead of us.

There were Kanduu and Kandeel, the outline of their bodies hazy and indistinct at the very edge of the light, doing just what we had rehearsed: scuttling back and forth in the hallway. If you knew about their alien chameleon skin, you could just barely tell that they were assuming the dark color of the walls and blending in, then sliding along until they popped out at a different place, taking on the lighter tone of the floor as they scampered across the hallway.

But to Joe and Sue Maxwell, it must have looked like a whole group of little kids was walking right through the walls.

Ghost kids.

This time the gasp did not come from Amy.

Did that mean they were buying it so far? I snuck a backward peek.

Sue was merely frowning, straining her eyes to try to make out what was happening in the hallway. But Joe had his fist pressed up against his mouth, and his arm was trembling a little.

I advanced slowly, careful to keep the little aliens right at the edge of the light. They dashed back and forth, perfectly maintaining the illusion of going through the walls. The Maxwells crept forward with us. It was so quiet that I think we were all holding our breath.

And then Kandeel started laughing.

Great. She picked a perfect time to get even more comfortable on this planet. She was going to ruin the whole thing before it really got started.

I knew I shouldn't blame her. After all, she was just a little kid alien, and I was the one who had put her up to this. She probably thought it was pretty funny to be chasing her brother around in the dark. I sighed. I guess we'd have to figure out another way to—

There was that gasp again. I turned. Joe Maxwell was chewing on a couple of his knuckles. And Sue looked a little more uncertain than she had a minute ago.

Amy reached up and switched the lantern off. And then I got it. Kandeel's squeaky little giggle, echoing in the darkness of a cellar at midnight, was extremely creepy. The kind of thing that would give people goose bumps if they were watching it happen in a horror movie.

I admit it: even I was kind of creeped out, and I knew what was happening.

The laughter faded. Silence settled all around us. When Amy snapped the lantern back on, the circle of light in the subterranean passageway was empty. Perfect.

"I don't think I can go any farther," Amy said.

I took a deep breath and let it out slowly. "Mr. and Mrs. Maxwell have traveled a long way to get here. We owe it to them to show them everything."

"You certainly do." Sue was frowning and craning her neck to see farther into the hallway.

"Actually," Joe Maxwell said, "I'm not so sure we need to see more of—"

Crash! Bang!

The cellar doors slammed shut behind us (courtesy of the Pink Blob and a couple of the alien kids who had been hiding in the bushes out back). Joe and Sue Maxwell jumped. (Okay, I jumped too.)

"Nowhere to go now but through the cellar," I whispered.

A low, rhythmic chant started up behind a closed door at the other end of the hallway.

30

As we made our way down the hall, the chanting intensified. I hurried past the closed door, Amy clinging to me, but Sue stopped. "What's supposed to be going on in there?"

I shook my head, not looking back. "You don't want to know."

"Let's listen to him," Joe Maxwell said. He grabbed his wife's hand and attempted to pull her past the door, but she dug in her heels.

"No way, mister. We're going to get to the bottom of all of this." She reached for the doorknob.

I hurried back, the light seesawing crazily from one side

of the darkened hallway to the other as the lantern swung in my grip. "I wouldn't do that if I were—"

Sue pushed the door open and the chanting got louder. The Arkamendian Air Painters were using their native language, so it sounded (I hoped) like ancient priestesses or whatever using some long-forgotten language. Very creepy.

And the visual was even better.

They were completely covered in hooded robes and doing a slower, more somber version of their floaty circle dance around a "cauldron" (actually a cast-iron smelting pot we had found in the storage shed). The bottom of the cauldron was lined with candles, so the reedy aliens were lit ominously from below.

And their creations looked perfect. A tangle of dark shadows rose from the cauldron and swirled around the room in time with the rhythm of the chanting. For all the Maxwells knew, a group of restless spirits was being summoned from the Underworld. At least that's what I was shooting for.

Some of the shadows emerging from the cauldron curled toward the ceiling and roiled there like storm clouds while others streaked along the walls, spinning around and giving the entire room an evil-kaleidoscope vibe.

Our little group stood there gaping at the eerie scene until a few of those floating ribbons of gloom came straight at us. We ducked as the living shadows shot over our heads and drifted down the hallway.

Amy dug her fingernails into my arm (a little too convincingly, I might add) and cried out in alarm. That was the Arkamendians' cue. All of their heads shot up and they looked straight at us. The chanting cut out suddenly, leaving an eerie silence.

The cowls of the robes hid their faces in darkness, but that just highlighted their eyes. They were glowing red. A dozen pairs of devilish eyes fixed us with unwavering stares.

One of the Arkamendians shot her arm straight out to point at us, and she spoke in that raspy, radio-just-out-of-tune voice. The message was a simple one: "Get. Out."

Joe thought that was a great idea. He grabbed the knob and started to pull the door shut just as the Arkamendians sent a rush of shadows straight for us.

Joe slammed the door, but the ribbons of darkness curled up from the crack underneath the door and swirled all around us. We sputtered and beat at the air with our hands, breaking up the shadows into puffs of dark smoke that lingered menacingly in the narrow hallway.

I rushed forward, holding the lantern out in front of me, and now even Sue hurried right along behind us.

We turned a corner, and this time *I* let out a cry of alarm, even though I knew what was coming.

Cottage Cheese Head, cloaked in dark material, looked just like he had that time when he'd accidentally scared me in the middle of the night—a glowing head floating down the hallway.

He looked right at us. "The living must beware..." he croaked, "the Hound of Hell!"

Snarffle raced past him and started chomping on everything in the cellar. Boxes of rusted junk, a stack of moldy magazines, an old tire; all of it ripped apart by his powerful teeth and gulped noisily down his cavernous gullet. It looked like he could eat the entire house. (At least that part of the show was true.)

"The Hound of Hell consumes everything in its path!" (The warbly delivery was a little too over-the-top theatrical for my taste, but whatever.) Snarffle continued to chomp and slurp his way through the piles of junk. He might've been smiling—I think he liked his new nickname—but I was hoping the Maxwells wouldn't notice.

Cottage Cheese Head brought one pale white hand out from underneath his dark robe so that it looked like disembodied fingers pointing in the opposite direction down the hall. "Go! Save yourselves from his hideous appetite. Save yourselves!"

I grabbed Joe's arm, and Amy latched on to Sue, and we took off. If we stayed there for one more moment I was afraid that they'd see past the gaping mouth and chomping teeth and notice that the Hound of Hell looked like a purple beach ball. (We had tried to put a costume on Snarffle, but he just kept eating it.)

We zigged and zagged around corners, turning down different hallways.

Suddenly I stopped. The corridor dead-ended at a brick wall, and standing there were the slime-drippers. They were down on their knees, wailing and moaning.

When they saw us they lifted up their hands, rivulets of slime dripping down their arms and pooling on the floor.

"Help us! Please!"

"We want to join the world of the living again!"

I spun around and blundered through our little group to get out of the hallway.

"What was happening back there?" I heard Sue say in the dark as the group speed-shuffled along behind me.

"They were covered in ectoplasm!" Joe answered.

"What is that?"

"It's a substance supposedly created when spirits cross over into the physical world."

"*Supposedly?* That looked pretty real to me."

"Will you two be quiet?" Amy whispered. "I don't want them to follow us."

I rushed around a few more corners. To the Maxwells, I hoped that it seemed like mindless, terrified running. But I was actually herding us toward our final scene.

Unfortunately, I found the right hallway by smell. I know it sounds stupid, but I didn't realize that ketchup would be so stinky when you dump out that many bottles. Hopefully Joe and Sue would be too freaked out to notice.

Ketchup was splattered across the floor in bright streaks. It was smeared along the walls in red handprints. It was pooled in the corners.

"Oh, my word!" Sue cried.

I turned and swung the lantern around and saw the Maxwells standing perfectly still, clutching each other. Now for the final surprise to send them over the edge....

I leaned against the wall for support and held up the lantern, the light playing across all of those red puddles. "This ... this is the reason the house is haunted," I breathed. "Something terrible happened here many years ago, and ever since then—"

Crash!

A ketchup-stained door flew open in front of us and banged against the wall.

The father from the body-parts-switching alien family

stood in the doorway...one fist gripping a handful of hair so that his head dangled below.

He raised his arm stiffly and lifted up the face so the eyes stared right at us. "What have I done?" his disembodied head wailed. "Oh, what have I done?"

A screechy sound right out of a horror movie filled the room (courtesy of Mrs. Crowzen, who was hiding in the closet and doing that thing with the bumps on her chest plate), and flashes of "lightning" (Crowzen again, operating a strobe light) lit up the scene.

The torsos of all of the alien family members were lying around the room...completely covered by a pile of twitching arms and legs. Oh, and completely covered in ketchup too. Lots of red, runny ketchup.

Amy screamed. It was a good one.

But then I noticed that a couple of the kids inside the room were smiling. And a few of the dismembered hands were waving to us. I lunged to slam the door shut before Joe and Sue Maxwell noticed.

This was it: the moment of truth. We had shown them every horrible detail of the "haunted" house, and now this was the part where they were supposed to run away screaming and never come back.

I turned to look at them. They were frozen to the spot, staring at the ketchup-smeared door. But they weren't running away. I was kind of hoping that they'd be running away by now.

Someone coughed behind the door with the red streaks. It was a very normal, everyday sound. Not a scary sound at all.

Sue tilted her head to the side, listening. There were

whispers coming from behind the door now. The aliens were probably wondering when they could put their limbs back on and wash off all that smelly ketchup. Again, not a real scary sound.

I looked a question at Amy, but she just shrugged. What were we supposed to do now? I guess we hadn't really rehearsed our exit strategy. It's not like we could just politely show them to the front door as if they'd been visiting for tea.

The entire future of the Intergalactic Bed & Breakfast hung in the balance. If we stayed down here much longer, all sorts of holes would be poked into this increasingly flimsy illusion we had set up. The slime-drippers were going to run by, laughing, or the Arkamendians would make brightly colored rainbows that would swirl around and cheerfully light up the whole cellar, or Snarffle would race down here to start licking up all the ketchup. He'd probably nuzzle up to Sue in the hope that she would scratch the blue dots on his rump. From what I've read, Hounds of Hell are not really known for that type of behavior.

I didn't know what to do. Why do my plans never work out the way I want them to? I was so flustered that I was just as frozen as the Maxwells.

But it didn't matter. Because just then the worst possible thing happened.

The circle in the middle of the door at the end of the hall began to glow a bright blue, and the last active transporter hummed to life.

31

The glowing blue circle started to pulse, getting faster and faster in time with a high thrumming sound. A cloud of steam seeped from underneath the door and curled toward the ceiling. There was a faint *whoosh* sound. The door began to ease open.

We all stood there and stared.

I realized that whatever kind of Tourist walked (or crawled or slithered) out of that transporter, it would ruin any slim chance we still had of pulling this off. When the Maxwells knowingly made their first face-to-face contact with a real space alien, they were going to see right through our plan.

We'd never be rid of them, or their UFO-obsessed network of friends. And Grandma would never forgive me. I knew it was really the end for the B&B this time.

I couldn't have been more wrong.

The thing that came out of the transporter was a monster, far scarier than anything we could have dreamed up for our fake haunted house.

It had a huge black body and a demon-red face. It came barreling out as if it had been shot from a cannon.

The bizarrely shaped body seemed to take up the entire hallway. And it was coming straight for us.

We all turned and ran, and there was no need to act anymore. All of the screams were genuine. (Yes, even mine.)

I lost my sweaty grip on the lantern handle, and we were swallowed by the darkness. The monster was roaring behind us. It might even have been using words, but I was too terrified to make them out.

My foot crashed into something and I tripped, but my body was painfully stopped short before I ever hit the ground. I realized that I was sprawled across the cellar stairs.

The wind had been knocked out of me, but I managed to croak, "Over here. This way."

The others nearly ran right over my back in their rush to escape. We stampeded up the steps together, and when the four of us banged into the doors with our shoulders, they gave way. We crawled out of the cellar and back into the moonlight.

As soon as our little group was out and on the lawn again, we turned, slammed the cellar doors shut, and sat on top of them.

Joe and Sue Maxwell looked at us, their terrified faces shining with sweat. Joe had lost his toupee somewhere and I didn't need any secret government machines to read his thought rays: *Get us out of here!*

Sue opened her mouth to say something, but just then the cellar doors lifted an inch underneath us before slamming back down again. The monster was trying to smash its way out.

"Okay, okay, we believe you!" Joe cried. "Now, how do you make it stop?"

Amy and I didn't have to pretend to be completely freaked out. "We don't know!"

Sue grabbed Joe and pulled him off the doors. This time —with only Amy and me holding them down—the doors lifted a good two or three inches when the monster smashed into them from below.

"Where are you going?" Amy cried.

"You can't just leave us!" Man, I never thought I would say something like that to someone like them.

"Yes we can!" Sue cried. "And we're never coming back!" She pulled on Joe's arm until he finally turned away, and they ran off into the night.

The cellar doors crashed upward a few more times, Amy clinging to me in terror, before they finally settled.

We could hear the terrible space beast wheezing below us. Was there a chance it was getting tired?

"What in the Sam Hill is going on up there?" a voice called from the cellar. "Let me out of here right this durn minute!"

Amy looked at me, then down at the doors.

"Dad?"

We stepped off of the doors onto the lawn, and Head of Security Robert Tate made his way out of the cellar. The leathery porcupine-quill things bounced all over as he climbed each step, and the black-feathered headdress framed his huffing and puffing face.

We all just stood there for a few moments, staring at each other.

Tate looked at our shocked faces, then down at his alien outfit, then back up at us again. "Don't say a word. Not one word."

Thankfully I was still too jacked up on adrenaline and terror to laugh. I just nodded.

Tate motioned toward the cellar. "Just what were you two doing down there, anyway? Who were those people? Why are there Tourists lurking around down there? And just why in tarnation would you—"

Amy stepped forward and hugged her dad fiercely around his big midsection. He stopped the interrogation and wrapped his arms around her.

"It's so good to see you again, Daddy," Amy said, her face pressed up against that sleek, shiny (and very stretched-out) material. "I was worried about you."

Tate leaned down and kissed the top of her head. "You too, sweetie."

"How did you make it back?"

Tate exhaled heavily. "Well, it turns out they had an emergency transporter on that dang cruise ship after all. I managed to get in touch with someone from security and explained who I was." He shook his head and looked up at the sky. "Finally found someone who was properly impressed with the fact that I work for the Intergalactic Police Force," he muttered.

Amy squeezed him even tighter. "However you did it, I'm glad you're home." Eventually she pulled away and looked up at him. "But I think that maybe *Don't say a word* should go both ways, okay?" She patted his outlandish costume. "It looks like we've both been through a lot. But you're home safe, and we're okay, and everything at the b-and-b is fine." She hugged him again. "So maybe no questions this time. Okay?"

Tate fixed me with a long stare. Too long. His eyes bore right through me. I started to sweat. I hadn't been this freaked out since...well, since five minutes ago, when he burst through the transporter looking like a monster.

Finally he took a deep breath and his glare softened a little. "Thanks for taking care of the place while I was gone, David." He looked down at Amy for a moment, then back at me. "And thank you for being there for my daughter. I appreciate it."

I discovered that I was able to breathe again. "You're welcome, sir."

Tate gently put Amy at arm's length and cleared his throat. "And, uh...speaking of not saying a word, that's actually not such a shabby idea. And, you know, maybe we should just keep all of this between ourselves when your grandma gets back." He studied the ground for a moment. "What do you kids think of that?"

I thought that was, by far, the best idea that Tate had ever had. "No reason to ruin her vacation, right?"

"Exactly." He cleared his throat again and scuffed his foot along the grass. "Besides, she's probably having so much fun on her off-world adventure that this place will have lost some of its shine for her. We don't need to trouble her with the fact that I raced off the planet to look for her, or with how I might have been dressed when I got back, or with"—he gestured down the cellar steps—"with whatever you kids have been up to."

"Don't worry, Dad," Amy said, patting him on one shiny black arm. "I'm sure she'll be glad to be back. She loves it here. And I'm sure she loves working with us, no matter how many amazing life forms she meets from around the universe."

"Well, I sure hope so," said Tate. "Because I—"

I never got to hear the end of Tate's thoughts on the matter, though, because just then a commotion kicked up behind him as all of the Tourists made their way out of the cellar.

"Did it work?" Cottage Cheese Head said.

"Did they leave?" the Pink Blob asked.

I nodded. "Yep, and I think they're gone for good. Thanks so much for helping us out, everyone."

The Tourists cheered while the kids swarmed around Amy and me, firing off questions.

"Did our slime freak them out?"

"Did I slam the door at the right time?"

"I heard them scream. That's good, right? Humans do that when they're scared?"

We laughed and gave everybody high fives and told them they were great.

Amy reached out and squeezed my hand. One of the little girl aliens stepped closer, peering up at us. "Are you going to mash your speech organs together again now?"

"They certainly are not," Tate said.

Snarffle raced around our little gathering, sniffing and smiling and licking and slobbering. When the kids tired of asking questions, they surrounded the little purple guy and scratched him all over. They didn't seem to mind the splotches of ketchup on his face.

Kandeel appeared beside me and took my hand to pull me down to her level. She was looking at the ground. "Sorry I laughed, David. I hope I didn't ruin your scary house idea."

"Are you kidding me?" I picked her up and cradled her in one arm, and she turned the same color as my T-shirt. "You were the creepiest part of the whole thing."

Her whole face lit up. "Really?"

"You bet. Even I was scared." That cracked her up.

While we were all standing out on the lawn under the full moon, telling war stories about how we had performed in the cellar, Mrs. Crowzen sidled up to Tate. "Ooooohhh," she said, looking the big man up and down, "this is the latest fashion design to come out of the Sarlazian Galaxy. However did you get your hands on it?"

"Is that some kind of a joke?" he spluttered.

"Of course not." She rubbed her claw along the sleek material of Tate's outfit. "It's gorgeous." Is it possible for crunchy exoskeleton crab plates to blush? Because it sort of seemed like it. "Why, I'm seeing you in a whole new light," she said shyly.

Tate's cheeks puffed out and turned red again. He looked right at me. "This is one more thing we don't tell your grandma, understand?" Then he stormed up the back porch steps and into the house.

Amy looked over at me and—with the tension of protecting the B&B finally broken—we both burst out laughing. We went on for a long, long time. Amy laughed so hard her knees went rubbery and she collapsed against me for support. I propped her up and we half-hugged and laughed out all of the stress of the past week. The aliens chuckled along with us, although I'm not really sure they knew why.

After wiping laugh tears out of my eyes and catching my breath, I nodded toward the cellar doors. "Let's get those closed up. We have a lot of cleaning to do, but we should probably wait until the morning." Now that the ordeal was over, I desperately needed to sleep.

Something was tugging at my shirt. I looked down, and there was Kanduu trying to get my attention.

"What's up, big guy?"

He looked at me very seriously. "You've taught me one very important thing about Earth."

"Oh, yeah? What's that?"

He rubbed at those segmented ridges over his belly. "We're going to need a lot of corn dogs to clean up all that ketchup."

33

When I woke up the next morning, bright sunlight was streaming in through my bedroom window, a somewhat unusual sight in the Pacific Northwest. But even stranger were the smells drifting up from downstairs. Coffee. Baking bread. Hash browns on the griddle.

The house hadn't smelled like that since the day when—

I jumped out of bed and raced through the empty hallways and down the stairs. I pushed open the swinging kitchen door, and there she was.

"Grandma!"

She's usually the big hugger around here, but this time I grabbed her and kind of swung her around.

She threw her head back and laughed. I finally set her down and she stepped away to take a look at me.

"Well, my stars and comets, that was quite a greeting, David. We were almost dancing."

"I'm really glad you're back."

"I must admit, I was beginning to wonder if anyone actually missed me." She gestured at all of the empty chairs around the big communal dining table. "Where is everyone this morning?"

"Probably sleeping in. We all had kind of a late night."

"I see." She tilted her head and gave me sort of a funny look. "Care to tell me about it?"

Um, not really. "I'd rather hear about your adventures. I'm sure they're much more exciting. When did you get in?"

"Just a few hours ago. Let me get us some refreshments and we'll have a nice chat."

Grandma made some hot chocolate for me and poured a cup of tea for herself, and we sat at the table. She told me all about her off-world trip: what the planet was like where she had stayed, the kinds of things she ate, all of her new friends. She said that she set up a referral system with a bunch of intergalactic hoteliers, and I got the impression that we were about to get even busier around here.

Thankfully we'd be able to run the place without the international community of UFO watchers looking over our shoulders.

The whole time Grandma was talking, her face was almost glowing. She usually looks pretty youthful—especially for a grandma—but this new excited shine in her eyes made her look almost like a kid again. Clearly, getting off the planet had been good for her.

I glanced around and noticed the same old walls that she had been looking at for over forty years of the B&B's operation. It made me think of something that Tate had said last night.

"So...you're really glad to be back? You promise?"

"Of course." But her smile faded as she studied my face. "Is anything the matter, David?"

Yes. "Not really." I traced the patterns of wood grain on the table. "It's just that...I don't know, we thought that maybe it would be so fun out there, mingling with all of those aliens from all over the universe and not having to hide any big secret...that you would, you know...not really want to be back here exactly. Or whatever. You know?" I'm obviously pretty articulate when it comes to talking about feelings and stuff.

Grandma reached out and placed one of her soft hands on top of mine. "I did have an amazing time, that's true. But this is my home, David. With the family and friends that I care most about. And this is where my life's work is."

I nodded. "That's good." I had to admit that was a big relief. Clearly the Tates and I weren't anywhere near ready to run the B&B without her.

She looked around the kitchen—at those same old walls —and sighed. "There is one thing that I wish were different, however...."

Uh-oh. Here it comes.

"The other hoteliers that I met were from more advanced

societies, so they didn't have to hide their operations from the general public. They are all fully integrated as contributing members of their communities." Grandma shook her head sadly. "The only real regret I have is that I don't think I'll live long enough to see all of this become public knowledge." She gestured at the entire house around us. "It seems so silly, especially after the week I've just had. We can all learn so much from each other. And have such a good time together. It's a shame that humans have to remain separated from all of the amazing creatures of the cosmos."

"But you're still glad to be back, right?"

Grandma laughed. "Of course." She got sort of a dreamy look in her eyes. "What I wouldn't give to see the good people of Earth mingling with my Tourist friends, just once." She took another sip of her tea and sighed. "Oh, well. We can't have everything we want. I suppose I'll just have to accept the fact that it's not a sight I will ever get to enjoy."

Wait a minute....

"No you won't!" I stood up so fast that I knocked my chair over. Then I took her by the hand and pulled her into the sitting room.

"David, whatever are you—?"

"Sit right here," I said, leading her to the couch.

"But why are you—?"

I ran out to the storage shed. After I found what I needed, I raced back inside. I set Tate's security camera on top of the TV and started hooking up wires.

"What are those?" Grandma asked.

"It doesn't matter. Just hold on a minute." I got everything connected and then turned on the TV.

"David? What is this? What's going on?"

I didn't answer; I just pressed PLAY on the camera and sat down next to Grandma on the couch.

The screen flickered to life and all of a sudden we were watching the Pink Blob stroll down Main Street, not wearing any disguise at all, high-fiving the citizens of Forest Grove.

Grandma's mouth slowly dropped open. "How did you...?"

"Don't worry—your secret's still safe. I'll explain later. Just watch."

Grandma slowly turned back to stare at the TV.

There were the ladies from the knitting place, making a fuss over dressing up a beaming Mrs. Crowzen in their homemade shawls.

Cottage Cheese Head held Snarffle's leash as a crowd of kids patted the little purple alien while he wriggled all over with happiness.

A line of alien kids stuffed their faces with ice cream as the crowd of laughing humans cheered them on.

And there were Grandma's favorites, the Arkamendian Air Painters, dancing in the Forest Grove town common out in the broad daylight for everyone to see and enjoy.

A tear leaked out from underneath the oversize pink lenses of Grandma's glasses. She reached over and squeezed my hand. "This is the most wonderful thing I've ever seen in my entire life."

Very cool. Especially considering some of the things that she had seen around here. "Consider it your welcome-home present, Grandma."

Everyone else in the house—human and alien alike—slept in really late. Grandma and I had all morning to sit together and watch the people of Forest Grove happily mingling with her guests.

Yep, it was another perfect morning at the Intergalactic Bed & Breakfast.

ACKNOWLEDGMENTS

It says my name on the front of this book, but I wish there were room for the following people:

My wonderful first readers Linden McNeilly, Trent Reedy, Katie Mathewson, and Myra Smith.

Chuck and Sue Robinson, Christina Claasen, and everyone at Village Books.

Bethany Hoglund, Bernice Chang, Jan Brandt, Helen Scholtz, Lesley Norman, Janet Peterson, and everyone at the Bellingham Public Library.

To all of the librarians, teachers, and children's booksellers who brought me in to talk to their young readers or put my books into the hands of kids, thank you for all you do. (I love you.)

George Nicholson, Erica Silverman, Caitlin McDonald, and everyone at Sterling Lord Literistic.

Christian Slade (his amazing illustrations are evidence that he must have found some sort of portal where he can peek into my mind and view my imagination).

Logan and Cameo, for laughing and cuddling and reading so many books with me.

During my years of receiving rejection letters, my agent told me, "It only takes one person to fall in love with your writing to change your life." Boy, was he right. I'm so grateful that one person for me was Stephanie Owens Lurie. Many thanks to Stephanie and her entire team at Disney•Hyperion.